THE FAR
MOUNTAINS

Other Little Dreams Books

Were You Still Dreaming, Ruby?

Red Ted

Billy the Brave

Robert the Frog

THE FAR MOUNTAINS
STEVE McGLAUGHLIN

LITTLE DREAMS BOOKS

MELBOURNE

LITTLE DREAMS BOOKS

www.littledreamsbooks.com.au
This edition published in 2025
ISBN 978-0-6487955-4-4
Copyright © 2025 Steve B McGlaughlin
Cover design by Nada Backovic
Cover photo by Aaron Burden on Unsplash

1 2 3 4 5 6 7 8 9 10

A catalogue record for this book is available from
the National Library of Australia.

Music can lift us out of depression or move us to tears –
it is a remedy, a tonic, orange juice for the ear. But for
many... music is even more – it can provide access even
when no medicine can, to movement, to speech, to life.
For them, music is not a luxury, but a necessity.

OLIVER SACKS

All I insist on, and nothing else, is that you should
show the whole world that you are not afraid. Be silent,
if you choose; but when it is necessary, speak —
and speak in such a way that people will remember it.

WOLFGANG AMADEUS MOZART

To Simone, Will, Josh and Holly.

CONTENTS

ARRIVING AT
STONE HILL FARM

When Robert was younger he lived somewhere else. When asked, he could never say exactly where, for the simple but painful reason that the nature of his removal from his home had been so sudden and rough and frightening, and had taken such a long time to end, that by the time he found himself in his new home and dared to open his eyes, he had not the slightest idea where he was or where he had come from.

In fact, the only details of his old home that he could remember with any confidence, were the last few minutes of his time there. Those minutes he remembered with a horrible clarity. Especially the voices of his mum and dad calling out to him and his siblings, who were playing on a

1

group of rocks in the middle of their large pond, "There's a big storm on its way! Get out of the pond now!"

Thinking back, Robert could not say if he had just been too slow to heed his parents' warning. It was entirely possible, for he was a boy easily captivated by the world. So it was likely he had lingered too long in the middle of the pond, looking at the black clouds which were, as his parents had urgently called out to him, "very, very dangerous, Robert!" But he could also remember why he had lingered: the clouds had a shape and colour that he found both beautiful and bewitching.

And it was not only how they looked that had held him there. It was also their sound – the most incredible, deep thunder claps, as if the sky itself was talking, wanting to tell him something extraordinary. So it was indeed very possible that he had stayed one or two moments too long on the rocks. But they were misjudged moments, that was all, not belligerent ones. Moments that were ruled by his heart.

However, the price paid for this delay, Robert now knew, was a truly terrible one. Even though it was only a handful of seconds, it was long enough that when he did finally dive from the rocks and swim as hard as he could to the bank where he could see his brothers and sisters clambering out, and his mother and father frantically urging him to hurry up, instead of a fresh surge of the storm's water missing him, it caught him up in its powerful grip, whipping him away at a speed he barely thought possible.

In the blink of an eye, he was swept to the far end of the pond, a place he and his brothers and sisters had never dared swim to before. Then, moments later, he crashed over the pond's embankment into the swollen river, which was flowing faster and higher than any living animal had ever seen.

Of the hours that followed this frightening separation from his home, Robert could not remember any great detail. It was as though all the rushing, falling moments had an endless, horrible sameness about them, like a gigantic jigsaw made up of only black pieces. The only thing he could say with any certainty was that he'd been lucky to survive.

For there were hundreds of dangerous items flowing alongside him in the river, any one of them capable of crushing, entangling or dragging him under at any moment. In the end, however, it was one such item - an old tree - which saved his life. When Robert speared into it, he was able to hang on to it, then crawl into an old hollow in one of its branches.

From that moment on, even though Robert still had to deal with the feeling that he was being swept further and further away from home, at least he had a sense that he could survive. So he said to himself over and over during that horrible night, "I am going to find my way back home. I am going to find my way back home."

❊

There passed an unknown amount of time, during which Robert would not have been able to tell you if he had slept or remained awake, for his eyes had stayed tightly closed. Then finally, he felt the tree slow down, then come to a standstill. "Where am I? Where on earth am I?" he thought to himself, alongside all manner of other frightening thoughts as to what might be waiting for him outside the old tree's hollow.

In the end, he knew the only way to find out was to have the courage to look. So after wriggling to the hollow's opening, then carefully poking his head out the top of it and looking around, the first thing he learned was that he couldn't hear any animals nearby. The second was that it was night-time. He knew this because the storm clouds had passed and the stars and moon were out.

The storm's end was a comfort. It was only a small comfort, but it was enough to give Robert the boost of confidence he needed to hop out of the hollow and onto the top of the branch. From here he was able to see in the moonlight that his life raft had become lodged in a clump of thick, tall reeds. When he looked around, he learned the reeds were a small distance from the edge of what seemed to be a large tree-lined pond that, in this light at least, did not look too different from his home.

This unexpected sameness finally caused Robert's most painful feelings – which he had been trying to keep away the entire journey down the river – to push to the surface and burst out. As his whole body began to shake, and he tried to hold back his tears, he said quietly to himself, "Please, just be a bad dream. Please, just let me be home with Mum and Dad."

But of course, this was not a dream, nor could he just magically go home. And it was only after accepting these two horrible facts that he sighed the deepest of sighs, one that might have come directly from his heart, and hopped back down into the tree's hollow to wait until morning.

THE FIRST FEW DAYS

The first two days and nights at the new pond were desperately hard for Robert, as he did not dare to step from the hollow for fear of the animals he might encounter beyond the reeds. From all he could hear, it seemed safe. But Robert had his father's voice in his head warning him, "For small creatures like us, Robert, danger can come in many shapes and forms. You must always be very careful when you are away from home."

But on the third day, when he could not stand his hunger pains any longer, Robert finally made the decision to risk swimming to the edge of the pond to look for some food. Being a strong swimmer, it did not take him long. And once there, he still did not see or hear anything dangerous, but he also did not find anything to eat. So he hopped onto the sand, then quickly through some thickly-leaved trees which lined the back edge. Once through them, he emerged onto a sandy path.

Here he made two important discoveries.

The first was the welcome discovery that just on the other side of the path was a group of familiar small plants that he knew would be a good place to find food. The second was that his new home was very different from how it looked from the reeds.

To the right, he saw that the land was made up of beautiful green plains sweeping as far as the eye could see. They were covered with many lovely tall trees, winding streams and a large variety of vibrant plants. But this view was not all pleasant and welcoming, for he also saw that the land was dotted with animals, big and small, who, although far away, still sent a shiver of fear through his entire body.

To the left and directly ahead, however, it was an utterly different story. There, soaring out of the ground only a small distance from the sandy path, was an extremely steep, wide hill, many hundreds of metres high. It was covered by a mixture of long spiky grasses, hardened small shrubs with twisted trunks, and other assorted plants robust enough to survive on such an open, exposed area.

But what set this sharp steep hill apart from anything Robert had seen before were the thousands of boulders, some small, many large, marking its slope. It was as though a giant's marble bag had split open at the top of the hill, spilling its contents down the slope. The hill's one saving grace was that there did not appear to be any animals on it, although Robert felt certain snakes and scorpions would be hiding amongst the boulders.

Robert was captivated by the unusualness of the rocks and the beautiful patterns they formed, exactly as he had been when he gazed up at the bewitching storm clouds. Only, this time he caught himself doing it, and began sternly chastising himself. "Stop daydreaming, Robert! Look how much trouble that has got you into already. What did Dad say? If only you had listened to him. Concentrate on finding some food!"

And it was a good thing too, for just as he was following his own advice by carefully hopping to the bush, he heard some leaves rustle, then a twig crack. "What was that?" he thought, freezing to the spot. "Please, please, don't be a big animal." But seconds later, he heard the same noises again, and when he looked up, his worst fears were realised, for it was indeed a big animal. To escape it, Robert leapt with all of his strength into the centre of the nearest group of bushes to hide.

The next set of moments seemed to tick over slower than a broken clock. They were terrible and frightening for Robert as he listened with sharp attention for the slightest sign the animal was going to attack him. But he didn't hear any more cracking twigs or rustling leaves, and knowing he couldn't stay in the bush forever, he dared to hope the creature had not seen him. So he slowly uncurled himself and peered out through the leaves.

"Oh no! There it is," he thought, almost blurting it out, which would have been a complete disaster, for it would have given away his hiding place in a second. "It is a big animal, and it is definitely trying to find me." Which was true, for the animal was standing very still, just a short distance away, scanning the bushes Robert was hiding in.

Seeing this, Robert knew he only had two options. He could hop onto the path as fast and far as he could and attempt to make it back to the Pond. Or he could rely on his green skin as camouflage. In the end, Robert chose the latter, because he had never seen a creature like this before and did not know how skilled and fast they were at attacking their prey. So he tucked his head back down again, hoping with his whole heart he had made the right decision.

But Robert had made the wrong decision. For he had forgotten something extremely important: like all his family, he had a very distinctive blue stripe running down the middle of his head, a marking which had caught the animal's attention in the first place.

As Robert lowered his head, rather than it offering him better camouflage, the stripe came back into full view, letting the animal catch sight of it again. But rather than immediately pouncing into the bushes, as Robert certainly expected it to, the animal - a human - called out in a warm, friendly voice:

"Oh! There you are, little fella! You know, you were not easy to find hidden in there." Then moving a little closer, with a wide smile breaking across his well-worn, tanned face, he went on, "I'm sorry if I scared you. But I'm glad you're here because I've never seen a frog with a beautiful blue stripe like that. And I've been looking at animals around this Pond for an awfully long time now."

Robert, of course, could not understand what the man was saying. He was not using the language other animals talk to each other in. But his tone of voice, and the way he remained crouching a safe distance away, made Robert feel he was not going to attack him, for the moment at least.

"I have a feeling that you are a long way from home, little fella?" the man went on. "I bet the big storm brought you here. Did you come from the mountains, all the way up there?" he said, pointing across the Pond to a mountain range in the distance.

"We've had all sorts of bits and pieces from up there over the years. But never a frog like you. Now, my little friend, please don't run away. I'd like to say hello some more this morning. But first, before this old head of mine forgets, I just need to finish the job I came down here to do."

With that, the man walked back along the path to a patch of long grass, where he crouched down and lifted a small cage. In it was a bright yellow bird. Robert's immediate scared thought was that he had been wrong in his judgement of this animal, and he might be next in the cage.

So, feeling that the big animal was both distracted and far enough away for him to out-hop it, he leapt back onto the sandy path. But when he landed, he looked up the path to check that the animal had not seen him, or worse, was beginning to chase after him, and he saw the man open the cage and put his hand in.

It was the gentleness in the way he did it that stopped Robert from continuing back to the Pond. He relaxed even more a moment later, when he saw the bird happily jump onto the man's open hand, and the man said, "It's time we got you back to your family."

And this big animal's kindness was confirmed beyond any doubt when, to Robert's surprise, after the man pulled the yellow bird from the cage and opened his hand, instead of flying away, the yellow bird stayed. It even inched its way up his arm. "C'mon, off you go. Your family will be missing you," said the man with a little more firmness, placing the yellow bird back on his hand. "You know you can come back here and say hello any time you like."

It wasn't until the man lifted his hand in the same way as one might assist a kite into the air, that the yellow bird finally flew to a high branch on a nearby tree. Once there, he called out his song, telling his family he was on his way home, then flew away. "That was a kind thing for that big animal to do," Robert thought to himself, now feeling a great deal safer.

But the next moment, something became very clear to Robert. For when the man absentmindedly, but with a sense of obvious enjoyment, whistled the yellow bird's call as he walked back down the path, Robert suddenly realised how he might be able to make himself safer yet in this strange new place. "I cannot understand this big animal's language," he thought to himself, "but I might be able to become his friend using the little yellow bird's."

So when the man was only a few steps away, Robert did his best to imitate the yellow bird's call. When the notes came out, they were not the same sound as the yellow bird's – after all, they were sung in a frog's voice. But whatever differences there were between his and the yellow bird's sound, there was also an obvious likeness that was easy for the man to catch. For, by fate or good fortune, Robert had stumbled across a man who had a deep passion for music. And for a moment, the man froze in surprise at what he had just heard this small frog do.

"Well, that was very clever of you," the man said, crouching down in front of Robert. "I have never heard a frog do that before. Never in my whole life. Wait until I tell Hennie about it! She'll never believe me. Maybe I don't even believe my own ears."

Then to make sure this event was not merely the product of his early morning sleepiness, or a trick of the music bouncing off the rocks in a peculiar way, he whistled the yellow bird's tune again. This time, however, he added a few extra notes.

Robert, clearly understanding that the big animal had understood him, repeated them back in perfect order and pitch. And the man laughed in such a joyful way – a sound understood across the whole world of animals – that, for the first time in three days, Robert felt his loneliness lift a little. He knew that for the time being, at least, he had at least one friend in his new home.

MONTHS GO BY

In the following days, from this very small but significant first meeting, the man always remained kind to Robert, seeking him out and talking to him most days. He was a farmer known across the district as Farmer Pat and, as he said he would, he did tell his wife, Hennie, about Robert. "She was just as amazed as I was, my little friend, and wants to come down and hear you one day. So you will have to promise to stay with us until then. Can you believe she had the cheek to say she's glad there's someone else I can share my singing with now, as her ears could do with a rest? That's a bit rude, don't you think?"

There were many conversations like this in Robert's early days at Stone Hill Farm. Robert looked forward to them as much as he could remember looking forward to anything he had before. For not only did he come to quickly love the gentle warmth of Farmer Pat, he was also able to use the confidence it brought him as energy, and a solid ground from which to begin to explore his new surrounds.

At first, he stayed close to his river branch in the reeds and the nearby sandy beach. But as the weeks and months passed, he became bolder and more at ease in his surroundings, and he explored more widely. From these ever longer journeys, he gradually learned that Stone Hill Farm had many wide-open spaces, but also many hidden little nooks. One, deep inside an old grey tree, became his permanent home.

Another of Robert's early discoveries was that despite the many differences among the farm animals - not least being that some liked to have the others for dinner – they all had two things in common. The first was that they all loved to talk and gossip down by the Pond. The second was that, like Robert, they were enormously fond of Farmer Pat, and were deeply attuned to his routines and rhythms around the farm.

As Robert was to learn, these rhythms began early in the morning when the animals would hear Farmer Pat's small blue tractor trundling down the long tree-lined driveway. It was a meandering, partly-sealed road, which led from his house on top of Steep Hill, all the way to a set of wooden gates at the far end of the property.

Most mornings, unless there was a problem from the night before, with his long-haired border collie Sam tucked up close to him on the driver's seat, Farmer Pat would travel about half way along the driveway until they reached a natural archway in the trees. Here the tractor would take a right-hand turn and bump down a rocky dirt track which ended at the entrance to what the animals called the Pond Paddock and where they waited for their morning food, head or belly scratch, or a friendly word. Even someone only at the farm for an hour or two, would not find it hard to see why the animals loved Farmer Pat as much as they did.

In those early days, Robert watched a great many animals mixing with Farmer Pat – cows, goats, sheep, geese, to name but a few – and then got to know them. Of them all, two were destined to become his best friends.

The first was Baz, a white duck who was, according to himself, on the larger side of middle-sized. Robert learned early on that he had not been able to fly since a terrible accident when he was a duckling.

"But…" Baz would add defiantly, each time it was mentioned, "do not feel sorry for me, Robert! I do not feel sorry for myself. I can waddle or swim as fast as anyone on the farm. Don't believe me? Well, on your feet and let's have a race!"

Like most of the other farm animals, Robert never took up Baz's challenges. So, to overcome his sense of rejection and still be able to demonstrate his waddling and swimming speed, Baz had appointed himself the farm's messenger. It was a "job" which allowed him to race across the grassy areas near the Pond, or fast paddle from one side of the Pond to the other, carrying the vital news of the farm.

Most of the time, the other animals regarded his "vital news" as pure gossip, largely about things he had no true business being involved in, or any real understanding of. But they tolerated his silliness, because on occasion, Baz did tell them something interesting or important, such as the time the old horse, Cassie, got her legs caught in the mud flats of the small dam.

In the early days, Robert, like most others, thought Baz funny and friendly, but still secretly or otherwise rolled his eyes at his big statements. But this view was turned inside out a few weeks after he arrived.

On that day, Robert decided to swim to the far edge of the Pond for the first time. Once safely there, he was quietly exploring a rock pool, until he was given a sudden enormous fright by a tremendous splashing noise. As he turned to dive underwater to escape from what he was certain was a hungry animal, he saw that the terrific noise was being made by Baz paddling as hard as he could across the Pond. Then, just a few moments later, it was made by his body as it stormed through the reeds, straight up onto the bank.

As Robert swung around to watch this spectacle of exaggeration, he suddenly realised Baz was not charging towards someone to deliver a message, but rather, at someone. And that someone was a large, orange fox slinking in the long grass, on the prowl for dinner.

At the same moment that Robert saw the camouflaged fox, it saw Baz. And when they became aware of each other and their eyes met, it was Baz who kept charging in a straight line, yelling: "Hey! You! Fox! Don't think I can't see you. What do you think you are doing coming around here? Find your dinner somewhere else! Go away! Get going! Off you go now – no need to dawdle!"

These words caused Robert's stomach to tighten into a small ball, and he blurted out loud, "Baz – what do you think you are doing? The fox will eat you!"

It seemed a hopelessly lop-sided contest that easily could have seen, as Robert said, Baz becoming the hungry fox's dinner. But quite against the odds, the fox turned and bounded away with its tail between its legs, not at all sure what kind of duck this wild white one was, or what it was capable of doing to him in this fit of obvious madness.

"Oh, Robert, were you there all along?" said Baz, desperately out of breath, when a few moments later, Robert called out to him.

"Yes, Baz, I was. I saw everything. I-I-I... have never heard of a duck attacking a fox before."

"Stop!" replied Baz with an unexpected abruptness. "I'm going to stop you there, Robert. Not another word. Please, not another word."

"But... it was incredible, Baz," said Robert, puzzled. "Really, it was."

"That may be so, Robert. But you need to understand I do not know why I did what I just did. The only thing I know is that I am already starting to regret it. Look at my leg," he said lifting up his trembling left leg. "Good grief – I'll never make it home."

"I think you did it because you were brave."

"Brave, is a big word, Robert! Too big. A word you would have to live up to if such a word was to find its way around to certain groups."

"But what you did was brave, Baz."

"But, Robert, the point is, I don't remember how I did it. So please do not tell anyone what you saw – they will expect me to do it again. Can you imagine what might happen? And now look at my other leg. It's shaking even more than the first one. I couldn't run if I had to. You see what I face? Let's head back now, in case the fox comes back."

"It won't come back, Baz," said Robert. "I wouldn't."

The other member of the small band of friends was Daisy, a fawn-coloured dairy cow with a lovely heart. She was a gentle, kind, dreamy soul, who loved nothing more than to slowly wander the paddocks, trailing her nose through the long grass in search of an eating experience she had once had years earlier. Her inability to ever recreate that "incredible grass eating day" was a topic she often returned to.

"Robert, dear, have I ever told you of the time…"

"Yes, Daisy, I think you might have already… a few… quite a few…"

"It was a spring day, just a normal spring day, quite like any other."

"Daisy, is this the story about the grass?"

"There it was, I could smell it first from a long way away, and its aroma was…"

"Perfect."

"That's right, Robert, it was perfect. Yes, I am obviously describing it well! The most perfectly delicious grass I have ever tasted."

"It sounds wonderful."

"Oh, but it was more than wonderful, Robert. It was stupendous. But it has never grown back. How could that be so, Robert? I blame myself. I should never have eaten it all. But it cannot only have grown once, can it? It has to be somewhere else. Doesn't it?"

"You would think so, Daisy."

"Yes, you would think so… I agree."

Like every other animal who knew her story, Robert would usually try and stop her endlessly retelling it, but in his heart he did not really mind how many times he heard it. For he quickly learned that it was a very nice feeling to be near the warmth that flowed from the story, and indeed, from Daisy herself.

So in those early few months at Stone Hill Farm, even though Robert did not have his family, he did have Baz and Daisy. And as anyone who has ever had anything to do with sadness or loneliness or troubled times knows, above and beyond anything else, true friendship is their best cure, particularly during the nights. So as he lay in his snug little home, Robert would often think to himself, "Of the places the wild river could have taken me, it was very good luck that it landed me here."

MUSIC AND THE STEEP HILL

Another reason Robert became such good friends with Baz and Daisy – apart from the simple fact that they just liked each other, found the same things funny and tended to have the same opinions on the quirks of other animals – was that they spent a great deal of time together in the evenings listening to the music Farmer Pat regularly played from his home. It would roll down the Steep Hill to the Pond below, winding its way through the boulders like a beautiful, searching mist.

On some days, the music could be heard around the Pond, but it was usually very faint, and could easily be drowned out by other animals such as the cicadas. But there was one special spot on the farm where it could be heard almost as clearly as if you were sitting outside Farmer Pat's home itself. It was a place Baz had accidentally discovered just a few weeks before Robert arrived, when he had been on the run from a formidable goose named Mrs Crichett.

"Why do you hide from Mrs Crichett, Baz?" asked Robert in the days after the fox incident, when he felt their friendship had established to the level where it was appropriate to ask a question of this kind.

"I won't lie to you, Robert. It's because I am scared of her. The whole farm is."

"They are?"

"Yes, particularly of her questions. Do not under any circumstances answer them," Baz said, as if giving Robert a valuable gift.

'Really? They're just questions, aren't they?"

"No, they're more like a spider's web. No matter how you answer the question - yes or no – it's always a trap that leads to stories about how hard her life is. The more you struggle to escape, Robert, the more you become entangled in them. Her bite is worse than a spider's, too."

"Is her life so hard?"

"No, not at all. She rules this farm!"

Robert, of course, didn't totally believe Baz. After all, he had already heard Baz's "vital news" enough to know that, while it was buried in there somewhere just like a shiny coin in a Christmas pudding, his truth needed digging and poking to be discovered.

So when he happened to bump into Mrs Crichett coming around the bend of a narrow path a few days later, and she said in what can only fairly be described as a neutral, courteous tone, "It's a nice night for a walk, isn't it, young Robert?" although Baz's warning arose in his mind, Robert still returned her courtesy and replied, "Oh, yes, Mrs Crichett, it's a lovely night for a hop now the sun has dropped behind the mountains and it's a bit cooler."

"Is it, Robert?" she replied, with a vocal abruptness matched by a physical one that caused her nine goslings to pile into her heels. If that reply was not enough to bring Baz's warning flashing out from the back of his mind, then her follow-up words certainly gave him the sticky, trapped feeling that he was starting to be entombed in a spider's web. "But how can it be, Robert, when…?" And just as Baz had warned him, this was merely an overture to three distinct movements of a great symphony of frustration and wing-wringing.

However, there was an unexpected reward for Robert's polite listening to Mrs Crichett's troubles and woes, which arose when he ran into Baz early the next day.

"I warned you!" Baz exclaimed. "And do you know, Robert, that if you had answered, 'No, Mrs Crichett, it's not a nice night for a walk', she would have said, 'Oh, but it is, young Robert – it has to be – who else is going to get some healthy air into these nine young bodies, to see to it that they grow to a good size?'"

"Don't listen to him, Robert," interrupted Daisy, who had wandered over and heard the end of Baz's rant. "She's quite harmless, really she is."

"She's a harm to my ears. And to my tail feathers."

"But you owe her, Baz," replied Daisy, with a hint of mischief in her voice.

"She owes me some tail feathers."

"Oh, Baz," Daisy went on, beginning to enjoy herself, "but you would never have found the hiding place without her."

"You have a hiding place?" asked Robert, curiously.

"We used to!" said Baz, rolling his eyes.

"Oh, you should come with us, and see for yourself," replied Daisy. "Don't you think, Baz? Robert would love it as much as we do."

"Oh... sure," responded Baz, "just so long as you promise to keep it a secret."

"Yes, I will – and I have," Robert replied quickly. "Remember on the other side of the Pond..."

"Ah! Let's not bring up that moment of madness."

"What moment of madness?" asked Daisy.

"Nothing, Daisy. All I was going to say was that Robert needs to be on the sandy bank when the sun is going down. Are we agreed?"

"Agreed," replied Daisy.

"Agreed!" added Robert, enthusiastically.

❋

Later that evening as the sun was setting, just as they had agreed, Daisy and Baz watched on as Robert swam from his home to the small sandy bank. Then with Baz leading the way, they walked along the same narrow dirt track where Robert had first met Farmer Pat and the yellow bird, and followed it for a long time as it meandered its way around the base of the Steep Hill. Eventually it became narrow and overgrown, before somewhat unexpectedly ending in a small open area, surrounded on all sides by dense walls of foliage.

"Oh, is this it?" said Robert, a little underwhelmed, as he had been expecting something a little nook-like. "It's…"

"We're not there yet!" replied Baz, thrusting his head into one part of the thick branches, then pulling it out again. "The hiding place is in there. Mrs Crichett would find us out here in a heartbeat. C'mon, let's keep moving before she does."

With that, Baz pushed his head back into the foliage, which seemed to Robert to just be leading into the hard rock of the base of the Steep Hill, until he saw Baz's whole body disappear.

"Stay close to me, Robert," said Daisy, pushing after Baz.

It was very good advice, for following in the wake of Daisy's wide body created an easy path for Robert; and after ten or so of her big steps – which was about twenty of his hops - the branches ended, and there before him was the opening of a lovely cool, sandy cave.

"Now this, Robert, is a hiding place," said Baz, flopping onto the ground. "Yes, it's very plain, I know."

"I wasn't going to say that it was plain," replied Robert.

"It is plain, but we still love it," added Daisy.

"But wait until the sun goes down," Baz went on, "just wait."

"There's nothing plain at all about what happens then," said Daisy.

"What happens then?" asked Robert.

"Better to have it as a surprise, Robert," replied Baz, using his whole body to smooth himself a comfortable spot in the sand, then flopping onto it. "Like it was for us. Until then, we relax. We're good at that, aren't we, Daisy?"

"We are," replied Daisy, dropping onto the sandy floor.

Soon enough, Robert too was nice and relaxed, knowing that he was safe in such a hidden space, with two bigger friends by his side. And so, with an extra sense of comfort, he was able to join in the conversation about the other animals, Farmer Pat, food, how much Robert missed his family, and any number of other topics they normally talked about.

But as it became dark, just as Baz and Daisy had promised, something surprising and rather wonderful happened. From a small opening at the end of the cave - which could easily have gone unnoticed, for it was no larger than one a human could stick their head into - almost like magic, out flowed Farmer Pat's music.

"This is how I discovered the Cave," announced Baz, proudly. "One day I was on the path hiding from Mrs Crichett, and I just suddenly heard it."

"But it is so loud and clear," said Robert, amazed.

"Daisy says it's almost as loud as if you were there on top the Steep Hill. Isn't that right, Daisy?"

"It's true, Robert," said Daisy. "It's completely true."

"Go on, Daisy, tell him then," prompted Baz.

"Once, before you came, Robert, there was a delicious scent and, if the truth be told…"

"Not the whole story about the grass!" interjected Baz.

"It's how it begins, Baz!" Daisy replied firmly. "And yes, I was looking for the delicious grass. But that day I became too excited. Really, it was my own fault. I should have taken more care. But my nose got too close to a fence. It was just a small scratch. But Farmer Pat brought me up to the barn, and Hennie put some cream on my nose and fed me some truly lovely hay. I could have stayed there forever, it was so nice. But from inside the barn you could hear the music just like this. And Baz is right, this is how the music sounds when it comes from inside Farmer Pat's house."

"Oh, it's just so…" replied Robert, captivated by what he was hearing.

"I find it lovely, Robert, just lovely," said Daisy.

"Oh!" said Robert, interrupting her, "this music is like what Farmer Pat whistles. Have you heard him?"

"You would know better than us, Robert," replied Baz. "All I know is, my legs never tremble when I am in here. When I come to think of it, I really should live here."

"We come here every time there's a warm wind," continued Daisy. "That's when the music comes down the hill."

"Oh, Daisy, look at Robert's face," said Baz. "I think he already loves it more than we do."

"That's because he can sing beautifully," replied Daisy.

"Oh, yes, I can sing," said Robert, "but this is far better than I ever could do."

There was no need for Robert to continue, for, as the others already knew from the way he sang from the branch above his home, it was obvious that this music meant a great deal to him. So it was agreed that from this evening on, when the warm wind blew, the three friends would meet on the Pond's bank, then slip away together along the sandy path to the Cave.

There were many of these warm evenings spent in the company of his two friends and Farmer Pat's music, and they were the best times of Robert's first year at Stone Hill Farm. Not only for the fun and joy of their friendship, and the warm feeling that arose in him when he was around them, but also because it helped him recover some of the strength and confidence he had lost when fighting for his life on the wild river.

But what Robert did not know, and could never have reasonably expected after all he had already gone through, was that he was going to need every part of this restored strength and confidence. For waiting just over the horizon, like impatient stars longing for the night to begin, was an even greater set of challenges which were going to make demands on every part of his courage.

WHAT HAS HAPPENED?

It was ticking into Robert's second year at Stone Hill Farm when for three days and nights, without rhyme or reason, Farmer Pat was nowhere to be seen or found.

As it happened, for the first two of these nights, the wind was blowing from the wrong direction, so the three friends saw no need to go to the Cave. Nor did they make too much fuss over Farmer Pat's absence from his morning rounds, knowing in their heads, if not their hearts, that there were any number of possible reasons for it.

But on the third night, as the sun sank lower on the horizon, and the wind blew steadily and warmly, the three friends did make the trip to the Cave, hoping they would find Farmer Pat's music, and that any small worry they might have been keeping from the others and perhaps themselves, could be cast aside once and for all.

✳

Long after it was dark, however, it was Baz who eventually said out loud what the other two were thinking. Though his attempt to sound confident and in control, as he had planned it out in his mind, was let down by a slight quaver at the end of the question: "Where's Farmer Pat's music?" A quaver he immediately tried to cover up by coughing.

"Oh, Baz…" started Daisy, her own voice beginning to quaver too.

"What? It's just the sand. It's caught in the back of my throat."

"Baz, you know how much I rely on you to stay positive," she went on. "Here we were, all having a lovely time, and you only have that to say."

"Daisy, there is no music. We aren't having a lovely time."

"Oh, but it still might be coming."

"It's pitch black! I can hardly see you. We should go."

"No, we shall stay. The music has been late before. We'll give it another few minutes. Until then, I insist that we all just sit here and think pleasant things."

"I really hope nothing has happened to Farmer Pat," said Robert, suddenly unable to keep his worried thoughts to himself.

"Robert! That's not 'pleasant things'! Why would you be like Baz? Nothing will have happened to Farmer Pat."

"Daisy's right - nothing will have happened," Baz went on, this time succeeding in his efforts to control his throat. But if there had been more light, Robert would have seen the telltale sign he was not telling the whole truth, because his legs were shaking.

"But how can you be so sure?" said Robert. "It's been three days."

"He's probably just gone to the Big Town," replied Baz.

"Yes, it's true, he sometimes does that," added Daisy. "Then that's it. He's in the Big Town."

"But I never saw the truck go up the driveway," said Robert.

"Robert!" said Daisy, "are you trying to make me cry?"

"Daisy, I promise he'll be down at the Pond tomorrow morning," said Baz, consoling his friend. "We'll hear the tractor. And all will be well."

"How can you be so confident, Baz?" said Robert.

"Robert! To prove how confident I am..." answered Baz standing up, then immediately thinking better of it, realising it would show Robert his true feelings, and so sitting down again. "If he's not, I'll spend the day with Daisy, searching for that grass of hers."

"Will you really?" Daisy replied, momentarily forgetting all about the whereabouts of Farmer Pat.

"Yes – but Daisy, don't expect we will find…"

"That would be absolutely wonderful, Baz. With your sharp eyes I have a feeling…"

"But Baz…" started Robert, trailing off because a part of him hoped that what he wanted to say was wrong. And he also didn't want to spoil Daisy's new sense of joy. But the fact was, ever since the terrible night in the wild river, it was as though he had an uncomfortable extra sense; one which, even when he would much prefer not to think about bad or worrying things, still arose to tell him when things were not what they seemed to be.

"You're worrying too much, Robert," said Baz, "really you are. Maybe you should make the music tonight?"

"What a splendid idea!" added Daisy, enthusiastically.

"No…" replied Robert, feeling that singing was the last thing he wanted to do.

"Why not? We've heard it when you sing back Farmer Pat's music to him," said Baz. "What's the difference?"

"Oh… it's just… Oh, I suppose I could…"

And to keep his friends happy, Robert did sing some of Farmer Pat's music. And while it could never hope to match that which came down the Steep Hill, it still made a beautiful sound inside the Cave. There was certainly no doubting Baz and Daisy's enjoyment of it, or that it did help to keep their minds from any thoughts about Farmer Pat, which they were trying very hard to keep away.

THE FOLLOWING MORNING

But while Baz and Daisy's hopeful, positive attitude helped Robert get through that evening and the night of hard dreams that followed, their way of thinking lost its power again first thing the next morning. For as the sun rose, Farmer Pat's blue tractor was, once again, nowhere to be seen or heard.

"This is not good, not good at all," Robert said out loud to himself, looking across the farm from his branch, hoping to see that with another day of proof, the other animals were now as worried about Farmer Pat's absence as he was.

But all he saw in their movement and routine was their seeming lack of concern and worry. As they normally did, the cows were heading in the general direction of the Pond Paddock gate without any great haste. It also seemed to Robert that none of the other animals, who usually might expect morning snacks from Farmer Pat, were hurrying out of their beds or moving nearer the Pond track to discuss their worries at not hearing the tractor for the fourth morning in a row. "But Baz and Daisy will have to have changed their minds," he consoled himself. "They must feel by now that something has gone wrong."

But after searching the regular spots for them - including the Cave - and not finding them, Robert took the risk of hopping to a small grassy mound in one of the smaller paddocks. Although it was exposed and made him vulnerable to the crows, he knew it would also give him an excellent view of the upper part of the Top Paddock.

Robert's risk paid off. For in a far corner, hard against the fence, he saw Daisy, nose down, slowly wading through a stretch of long grass. There too was Baz, riding on her back, vigorously pointing his wing in various directions. "Daisy really made Baz keep his promise," Robert thought to himself, an uneasy feeling flooding his body, for he knew that the low chance of finding the grass, combined with Daisy's powers of patience, meant his friends could be away the whole day.

Before his journey down the river, Robert may have just waited until they returned. But with his new "extra sense", that simply would not do now. So to help with his loneliness and worry, he began hopping around the safer parts of the farm, asking everyone and anyone, "Do you know where Farmer Pat is?"

The older animals were just the same as Baz and Daisy, and quick to reassure him with calm words such as: "Over the years, Robert, there have been many times Farmer Pat has not come down to the Pond for a few days." And: "We're sure he'll be here tomorrow, Robert – perhaps the tractor isn't working?" Or: "Maybe he is away on holiday in the Big Town?"

While a sweet cow friend of Daisy's told him, "Have you thought he might be spending all his time on the far side of the farm? We heard from the cows in the far paddock, who heard from the cows in the far, far paddock, that there is still a great deal to do after last year's big storm."

Every time Robert listened to these explanations, he wanted them to be true, and he tried hard to make them feel that way. But as soon as he walked away from the animals with their logical explanations and reassuring manners, his doubts rose again like water in a sinking boat.

And as the day went on, Robert began to understand that his best chance of finding an answer was from a bird. A bird was not locked behind the Pond Paddock's gate, or too small like himself, to risk journeying through the paddocks to the Stone House. So his hopes leapt when he happened to see one of his friends, a cockatoo, soar from the top of the Giant's Teeth, the long row of boulders which sat like a fortress wall on top of the Steep Hill.

This friend, Charlie, landed on a branch on the far side of the Pond. Just as Baz had on "the fox day", Robert swam as hard as he could across the Pond, and without even checking to see if there were any dangerous animals about, he hopped right up to the tree Charlie was perched in.

"Charlie!" he called.

"Oh, who is it…?" Charlie replied, distractedly, focusing his eye on a tough-skinned seed grasped in his claw, searching for any chinks in its armour that would make cracking it easier.

"It's me, Robert… I'm in the grass. Right below you."

"Oh, so you are, Robert," Charlie replied, edging down the branch, then cocking his head to one side to give himself a better view through the leaves. "You're certainly a long way from home, aren't you? It can be dangerous over this side of the Pond, you know. You should hurry home."

"Yes, I know, Charlie. But I need to ask you if you have seen Farmer Pat today. He hasn't been down to the Pond for the last four days. He hasn't been playing his music either."

"Oh, yes, his music – I sometimes hear it when I am sitting up there," Charlie said pointing to the Giant's Teeth. "It's quite wonderful, isn't it?"

"Yes, yes – it is!" Robert, went on anxiously. "But it seems to be gone, Charlie. That's why I was wondering… hoping…" but then he suddenly stopped, realising the question he was about to ask had two possible answers, and he wasn't sure how he would feel if he received the wrong one.

"Robert? The question?"

"Yes… I was wondering," Robert finally went on, "if you know where he is?"

"Oh… I…" said Charlie with a great deal of sympathy in his voice.

"You haven't seen him up there, have you?" Robert said, jumping in quickly, as though this might ease the blow of what might be about to come.

"I don't want to tell you bad news, Robert. I really don't. But the truth of the matter is I have not seen him anywhere lately."

"Oh, I see."

"But if it helps, Robert, I also haven't seen anything bad or wrong."

"Oh, Okay. Thank you, Charlie. Yes, that helps."

"Robert. I'm sure he is safe and well. But really, at this time, you should be hurrying along. I spend far too much time in the company of the crows on top of the Giant's Teeth to know just how much they would like to find you standing here like this."

Later that afternoon, after returning from their long day searching the paddocks searching for Daisy's grass ("not a long day, Robert, the longest day!") Baz and Daisy declared they were too tired to go to the Cave. And even though it was cool, and the wind was blowing from the wrong direction, Robert decided to go anyway.

41

In the clear, sensible part of his head, he knew that because of the weather, the music would not appear in its typical way. But in the back of his mind, he still had a secret hope that even though the weather was not perfect, Farmer Pat would decide to play his music on this night, just to let them know that he was back from wherever he had been, and everything was safe and well.

After Robert reached the Cave, he carried out the friends' normal routine of finding a comfortable spot in the sand and sitting down. The only difference was that this time he sat very close to the small gap in the rocks so he could be sure to hear even the faintest music should it appear.

But to his sorrow, even after waiting until the moon had risen well into the night sky, the music did not arrive. There were, however, other banging sounds from the top of the Steep Hill, which gave him moments of hope, but not a note of Farmer Pat's beautiful music.

As Robert sat in the pitch-black silence, lonely and scared, it became clear to him that if he wanted to know where Farmer Pat was, he was going to have to find out for himself. This conclusion carried with it two equally frightening, risk-filled options of how he might actually get to the Stone House.

If we were in a classroom, a teacher might ask us: "Children, can anyone tell me why it would be so difficult for a small frog to hop along a long, open road, or to climb a Steep Hill, by themselves?" We could imagine a sea of eager, knowing hands flying into the air. And when the teacher points to the hand that flew up first - or perhaps, because of the nature of the question, to the hand that rarely went up, but felt the need to push through their shyness because they felt they understood Robert's plight better than most - the first child might answer, "Because frogs are so small." And the teacher might have said, "That's a good answer," and written it on the board, then turned back to the class and pointed to the next child, to hear: "Because frogs are easily spotted away from green camouflage."

And when the teacher was encouraging about that answer ("yes, very good, very good"), the class might have kept going and added more to the list, such as: "They don't have claws or sharp teeth," or "… a ferocious growl to scare other animals away," or "they are not very fast compared to some others," or, "they have soft skin," or indeed, "they need to be near water."

After the teacher has written all these answers on the board – and possibly also many more – and it has been noted that it is a very large list with many reasons why frogs have to be exceptionally careful when leaving their home, well then, it is not unreasonable to conclude that every child would have thought to themselves or said to their friend: "Well, if that was me, I wouldn't just go hopping along a path, or climb through dark tunnels in rocks, as I might quite easily end up in the belly of a snake, stung by a scorpion or whipped away by a crow."

Of course, Robert knew all the reasons why he should not go, so he pondered for a long time whether he had the courage to embark on either of these journeys, or whether it would be more sensible to endure another painful night and day of not knowing where Farmer Pat was.

When he made his final decision, Robert hopped to the end of the Cave. Once there, he climbed into the small gap in the rocks, and waited until he heard one of the banging sounds from the top of the Steep Hill. He was going to use these sounds to guide him through the maze of rocks all the way to the top.

FINDING THE WAY

Anyone who knows anything about climbing mountains - that is, those who have read the right books, or have been lucky enough to have snuggled close to their grandmother or grandfather on cold winters' days and heard stories about "those who had climbed the mountains in the old days", or those who have climbed mountains themselves - will already have a sound idea of what the first part of Robert's climb up the Steep Hill felt like.

This is because everyone who has ever climbed a mountain feels the same inside themselves while climbing it. You have to accept, or come to terms with (as in Robert's case) the fact that there is no way of knowing what lies hidden in the tight, dark passageways between the boulders, but keep going anyway.

And it is not only one's fearful voices that need resisting. There are also the "sensible" ones that demand that you immediately turn around: "Why are you doing this, Robert? Farmer Pat is quite all right - the others were most sure of it." Or: "You will fall and hurt yourself if you keep going – it is a certainty." And the most compelling of all: "Robert, you should be leaving this task to a bigger animal; that's okay too. This is not a journey a small frog is supposed to be making."

But Robert never gave in to these voices as he scaled the first part of the Steep Hill, clambering over and between rocks, falling into crevices and holes, every part of his body on high alert, getting scratched, scraped and bumped, while continually looking up and around, just waiting, watching for the dreaded sounds of dangerous, hungry animals. Instead he fought them by saying little encouraging things to himself, such as, "Keep going, Robert. Think what your brothers and sisters would say. They would never believe you." And, "Imagine how proud Baz and Daisy would be, Robert."

In spite of this struggle, after many hours of climbing Robert found himself well past halfway up. And it was here, quite exhausted, that he decided to stop for a rest. As he searched for a safe, protected spot to sit down, he looked back down the slope to see how far he had come and happened to choose a moment when the just-risen moon was reflecting beautifully in the centre of the Pond. Even to Robert, an animal we already know to have a great sensitivity for beauty, this sight was simply the most glorious he had seen.

As he stared at the moon's reflection, it seemed to float and flicker, and be more part of the earth than the sky. And it also brought his attention to the reeds his raft had first become caught up in. This reminded him of all Farmer Pat's kindness which, like heavy rain falling in a river, brought with it a tremendous burst of fresh energy to finish what he had set out to do.

A short while later, Robert pushed his way through a particularly tight gap, then scrambled over a group of old, hard, leafless branches and found himself in an open patch of scraggy grass. When he looked up, he saw that his way was now completely blocked by a massive wall of boulders.

"Oh! I'm at the Giant's Teeth!" he said out loud, in a tone which would have told anyone who heard it that he was feeling a mixture of pride, relief and trepidation.

Which was fair, as Robert being at the Giant's Teeth was indeed a mixture of both good news and bad news. The good news was that this was the last hurdle before reaching the top of the Steep Hill. The bad news was that the Giant's Teeth were even bigger and more tightly packed than they appeared from down below.

But Robert had overcome many fears and obstacles, and he was not going to be stopped now by these massive rocks or what might be waiting for him on top of them.

"All I need to do is climb through a gap, and find a hiding spot on the other side until morning," he thought to himself. "That's all, Robert. Just a few more minutes. You can do this."

For the next five to ten minutes, Robert hopped along the base of the Giant's Teeth, searching for a way through that he trusted enough to feel that it wasn't going to lead him straight into a snake or scorpion's home. But to his great disappointment, even after doubling back on his tracks three times, he could only find gaps that he felt certain would lead to deep trouble.

This left him with only one alternative, which came with its own new set of fears: to use his good grip to climb up the side of one of these boulders, then hurry across the exposed top as fast as he could.

After accepting this was the only option left to him, he stood on his back legs and began scaling what he thought was the smallest of the Giant's Teeth rocks, gripping with all his strength, continually looking up and around for any sign that an animal had seen him and was coming to snatch him away.

But to his enormous relief, Robert made it up the steep side of the boulder without any sign of trouble. Then, spending what felt like the last drops of his courage, he carefully poked his head over the top. "There are no crows!" he thought joyfully to himself, dropping back down again to remain out of sight. "Now, don't do anything rash or silly. Remember what Dad told you."

But it was hard for Robert not to feel excited, because his quick peek over the top had also shown him two other wonderful things. The first was a thick group of trees which, from this short distance away, looked to offer a safe hiding place for the rest of the night.

The second, however, was far more thrilling. Just forty metres or so beyond the clump of trees, he had seen Farmer Pat's Stone House. "There's no giving up now!" Robert said to himself, feeling as though seeing the Stone House had given his energy and courage a gigantic boost. "It's only a few big hops away."

With that thought powering him on, he took a long, deep breath and lifted his whole body onto the top of the boulder. But before he could take even one hop, he was stopped dead in his tracks by the sight of the sky filling with the animal frogs fear most after snakes and crows: it was a flock of bats.

For many minutes, Robert, deeply frightened and bitterly disappointed, watched the bats stream across the sky in their strange, jerky way, all the time hoping that by getting used to seeing them, his fear would lessen. But despite all his efforts to push this ugly feeling away, he wasn't able to. It soon seemed to him that the situation was completely hopeless, and that he would just have to hide in this spot until the morning, when the bats would return to their homes deep inside the rocks.

As time went by, he wedged himself into what seemed a safe crevice, and began to notice that none of the bats ever seemed to be looking down at the Giant's Teeth.

"After all," he reasoned, "from a bat's point of view, it would surely be unusual and quite unlikely for a frog, or any small, tasty animal, to have climbed to the top of the Steep Hill ready to be whisked away and eaten." Also, he began to think, "Even if they were to see me, they would be so high in the air, and I would be too fast and have too good a head start across the rock, for them to catch me."

After more consideration, Robert made the decision to press on. So he climbed back onto the boulder, then took some very quiet, cautious, slow hops across the top of it, looking up after every one for the slightest sign that a bat had caught sight of him.

Now, perhaps it was Robert's very kind nature, which did not allow for just how cunning some hunters are, or perhaps he just did not know how clever bats were as hunters, but whichever it was, the cold truth of the situation was that Robert had already been spotted by one of the bats as it flew over him.

And as Robert was taking his first small tentative hops across the boulder, this bat had already turned around - having taken a long detour - and was coming for Robert from directly behind. It was now no more than ten or so wing flaps behind him, mouth open, ready to attack.

It is terrible to contemplate that Robert was not yet aware that he was in the greatest danger of his life - even greater than when he was struggling in the wild water in the storm in his home pond.

Up to that point, the bat had made his attack in the most perfect style. But then, whether through boasting to its friends, or in the excitement of being about to have an easy meal in only the first few minutes of its nightly hunt, or whether it was simply trying to cause Robert to freeze in terror, it unexpectedly gave Robert the smallest window of a chance to survive, and let out a truly frightening screech.

Robert took his chance. When the bat made its final lunge, snapping his jaws closed, expecting to bite down on its dinner, it found nothing but air. And this was because Robert was gone; he was falling from the other side of the boulder, bracing himself for what he was certain would be a horribly painful crash landing.

But thankfully, on this night the Universe had different plans for the brave little frog. Instead of crashing onto rocks, which may have injured him badly or, at the very least, cut his feet open making further hopping completely impossible, he landed between them, onto a soft ball of thick moss. While it knocked the breath out of him, as he lay there very still, he was able to see the stream of bats up above in the sky, and quickly realised that this hiding spot was too tight and narrow for them to fly into.

After a few minutes, when his breathing was back to normal, Robert climbed out of the small ravine. Then with one final look across the sky, he again took the risk and hopped as fast as he could towards the trees. This time no one chased him or attacked him, and he made it without trouble.

Once there, he rustled amongst the leaves as quietly as he could, until he found a small tunnel which led under the exposed root system of one of the trees. It would never have done as a permanent home, but it seemed safe enough for what was left of the night. And it was all the exhausted Robert needed right now. So with that small sense of comfort acting like a night guard, he tucked up tightly in a dark corner and promptly fell asleep.

THE STONE HOUSE

The following morning, the sun was only just rising when Robert, who had slept very poorly, found himself wide awake considering the unpleasant question: "How am I going to make it across the open ground to Farmer Pat's House?"

It was easy to see how he might do it, as it was no more than thirty good hops away, a distance that he could easily cover quickly. His problem, however, was the same one that had been haunting him the whole way up the Steep Hill - the question of what might be hidden out of view, waiting for a small frog to hop into an area where there were no places to hide.

After pondering this problem without coming to any satisfactory answers, Robert decided that the wisest course of action was to not take any action, at least for a while.

But, as seemed to be the case so often for Robert in this period of his life, just as he was settling back down into what he thought was a safe hidden place, his world became dangerous again. He heard the unmistakable sound of a large animal rustling its way through the undergrowth. "Oh, no! What is it this time?" he thought to himself, feeling horribly scared and tucking himself into the tunnel's furthest corner, praying it would not be able to find him there.

For the next few moments, it seemed that he was going to be safe, as the animal remained rustling and sniffing a short distance away. But then, obviously better locating Robert's scent, the animal began digging and sniffing with a far greater determination directly above him. This change forced Robert to make two of the biggest and most courageous decisions of his life.

The first was to decide: "I am not going back down the Steep Hill. I have come too far to turn back now. I am going to try and make it to Farmer Pat's House no matter what." And as if to protect himself from the awful possibilities of what "no matter what" brought with it, he kept himself brave with the thought: "There is a chance the big animal will not be able to see me as I hop through the leaves."

The second was a passionate promise to himself about what he would do if the big animal did see him and chase him. Here he took his inspiration from Baz. "I will not go down meekly. I will fight as Baz did with the fox. I am going to puff out my throat and stand as tall as

I can, then turn around and charge straight at this animal and yell at it, 'Go away! Get going! Off you go now – no need to dawdle. Find your breakfast somewhere else.'"

With those strong, angry, brave words in his head and heart, Robert felt a small surge of confidence. He used it to move closer to the entrance of the tunnel, where he poked his head out, saying to himself, "C'mon, Robert, you can do this." He didn't see the animal, so he hopped as fast as he could in the direction of the Stone House.

But almost immediately, Robert could tell he was in deep trouble. He had not hopped more than five or six times, when he realised that his hope that the fallen leaves would provide him some camouflage had not worked, because he could hear the animal chasing after him.

So, accepting he was just going to have to stop and fight as he promised he would, he puffed out his throat, stood tall, then turned and began shouting. But as he turned, instead of seeing a creature with its mouth open, teeth bared, ready for breakfast, and being filled with a horrible fear, he was filled with the most incredible rush of relief. For there, only a few metres from him, was Sam, Farmer Pat's dog.

"Oh, Sam! It's only you," said Robert, so relieved the words almost didn't make it out of his mouth, "I-I-I thought you were going to eat me."

"Robert? Is that really you?" replied Sam, astonished. "How on earth did you get all the way up here? I didn't quite know what I was digging for. But I can honestly say the last thing I expected was for it to be you."

55

This statement, delivered with genuine concern, was all the trigger Robert needed to let all the heartache and worry of the previous night and the days before burst forth in a stream of words and sentences which told Sam all the important and significant parts of the story. The final sentence was: "Sam, do you know what has happened to Farmer Pat?"

When she heard this question - particularly the tone it was delivered in, and the sincerity in Robert's eyes - Sam found herself in a truly horrible situation. One that every creature who lives a life full of friendships will once or twice find themselves in. "Oh, Robert..." was all she could get out before stopping herself.

Robert's question had placed her in a situation of deep inner conflict. Even though she had the answer to Robert's question, she held it back because of a feeling in her heart that if she were to deliver a full, truthful answer to her friend, he would be overwhelmed by it. So as she examined Robert's tired, scratched face and body, she decided to wait.

Of course, in her heart, Sam wanted to tell Robert everything. Which was that only a few weeks ago, Farmer Pat had taken Hennie to the Big Town. But when they had got back in the car they both had looked so terribly, terribly sad, and had barely spoken any words, only holding each other's hands on the way home.

After this visit - and there were more - Sam began to notice Hennie could not take her on their usual night walk for as long as usual. And the walks continued to get shorter and less frequent, until it reached the point where she could only sit on the back porch and watch on as Farmer Pat and Sam did a final check of the farmhouse surrounds before they went into the house for dinner.

This was what Sam wanted to tell Robert, more than anything. For when she had not fully understood what was going on these last weeks, it had left her feeling terribly lonely. But as she waited for the right words to form in her head, two big tears formed in her eyes and rolled down her cheeks.

"Sam, what is it?" asked Robert.

"Robert, it is easier if you come with me. I can show you what has happened to the music. But you will have to follow me to the big barn."

"Sam, if I hop into the yard..." began Robert, seeing the crows, who were now wide awake, talking amongst themselves on the Giant's Teeth.

"It's all right, I'll protect you. I promise you'll be safe," replied Sam.

Robert could see the crows looking at him, and he did not trust them, but he did trust Sam completely, and he knew she would protect him. So he hopped along under her legs until they reached the fence behind the big barn.

Once there, Sam dropped to her stomach, crawled under the fence, and then, because this side of the Steep Hill was a sheer cliff face, stayed on her belly until she reached the point where her front paws and head were over the edge.

"Robert," she called, turning her head to look back, "come carefully and look down here."

Robert hopped straight up to the edge, making Sam's heart jump hard; such that she swung her paw around, thinking that Robert might fall. But he had wonderful balance, and was soon lying next to Sam, leaning over the edge, looking down and trying to see what she wanted to show him. Eventually, he had to admit, "I can't really see anything, Sam. What am I supposed to be looking at?

"Right there," replied Sam, carefully pointing her paw, "over there. Next to the big round rock, with the tree growing out the top of it. Do you see the black box?"

"Yes."

"Do you know what it is?"

"No."

"That is the machine Farmer Pat used to make music. That is where the music lived. Or where it used to live. But now everything is broken. A few nights ago, when Hennie wasn't here anymore, Farmer Pat walked out of the house with the machine under his arm, and threw it over the edge."

"Oh, Sam…"

This was the moment when Sam knew she had to tell Robert the whole story of what had happened. And as she did, the tears began to roll from her eyes again, for this was one of those stories you have to tell a thousand times before being able to tell it without feeling the deepest sadness. It was a terrible thing to have to tell Robert that a gentle, kind and loving man like Farmer Pat had lost the person who was most precious to him.

*

After Sam had finished telling Robert about the last few days, which had ended in Farmer Pat throwing away his music, Robert and Sam lay there, very still, staring down at the broken music machine. They had a sense that saying nothing was better than any words they could speak.

Eventually, Robert ended the silence. "What shall we do, Sam?"

These were the right words for Sam to hear. For they brought out into the open the question that had been weighing heavily on her heart these past few days. What can we do? How can we help Farmer Pat? And beyond that, what is going to happen to Farmer Pat? What is going to happen to Stone Hill Farm? What is going to happen to the animals?

"Robert," she finally replied, sadly, "the truth of the matter is that I am not sure there is anything we can do."

60

NOTHING CAN
BE DONE

The way Sam had said those words swam around Robert's head all through that long, hot day. He had little choice but to hide under Sam's kennel, only cautiously popping his head out occasionally to see if any animals were in the area, and then if he felt safe enough, taking a quick swim in Sam's dog bowl to keep his skin cool and wet.

But as much as Robert dedicated his mind to how he or the other animals could help Farmer Pat, by the time the sun set and he felt safe enough to travel back down the Steep Hill to the Pond, he was no closer to an answer.

Luckily, just as he was about to begin to hop back across the open area to the Giant's Teeth, Sam pushed open Farmer Pat's front wire door with her nose. "Robert! What on earth are you doing?"

"I'm going home, Sam," Robert replied, stopping and turning around. "I wasn't sure where you had gone. Baz and Daisy will be worried."

"Oh, I'm sorry! I was inside with Farmer Pat," said Sam. "Now, you're most definitely not going down the Steep Hill, Robert. I am going to take you the long way, down the driveway and path."

"Oh, thank you, Sam. That would be much better."

✳

Robert was relieved by Sam's offer, for he never wanted to have to go up or down the Steep Hill on his own ever again. Moments later, they began walking and hopping down the driveway, with Robert staying very close to Sam.

"It's terribly sad, Robert," Sam said after a while, with great emotion in her voice. "Hennie was so lovely and kind to everyone."

"Yes, Daisy told me she looked after her when she cut her nose."

"I remember it. But it was not only Daisy. She looked after all the sick animals. Farmer Pat, too, of course. And she'd always give me a secret snack in the evening when Farmer Pat went inside to turn on the music machine."

"That would have been lovely, Sam…"

"Lovely and delicious! But I never had to worry that Farmer Pat would be upset his snacks were gone, because once the music started, he would always come back very happy, and give my tummy a good scratch. He was always singing or whistling along. It made Hennie happy as well. It's all so sad, Robert. I really don't know what we are going to do now."

"We'll all just have to look after Farmer Pat."

"Yes, that's right. And that's what we have been trying to do up here. We've been trying, Robert. Really, we have. But it doesn't seem to be working.

With those sad words, the two friends realised they were back in the same difficult place where they had looked over the edge at the broken music machine. Once again understanding that words were not of any proper use, they fell back into silence as they made their way down the path to the Pond Paddock.

"Thank you for coming with me, Sam," said Robert once they reached the gate. "I can make it home from here. I know all the hiding spots on the way to the Pond."

"Are you sure?" replied Sam, "I can easily squeeze under the fence."

This was not entirely true, as Robert had seen how Sam had struggled to get under the fence behind the barn, and this particular fence would have been quite a tight fit even for a younger dog.

"Sam, what can I tell everyone to do to help Farmer Pat?" said Robert, from the other side of the fence.

"We will just have to wait and see, Robert. That's all we can do. We're just animals. But I will send any news straight away," replied Sam, knowing that although this was a good thing to hear, she wasn't sure she was going to have any good news to send for a long time yet.

"Thank you, Sam," said Robert, "I will do the same. And if I hear of any ways anyone else can think of to help, I will get a bird to fly it up to you."

"Yes, anything at all… anything at all, Robert."

With that, they said their farewells, and Robert began hopping down the long track towards the Pond to find Baz and Daisy.

BAZ AND DAISY
FIND OUT

To Robert's great relief, it did not take long to find Baz and Daisy. After only ten minutes of careful, watchful hopping, he saw them on the sandy beach, looking up at his favourite tree branch. But just as he was getting close enough to call out to them, they suddenly hurried onto the path to the Cave.

As it happened, Baz and Daisy were only hurrying to the Cave for the first time, for it had taken the whole day for them to learn the news (via the bats to the crows to the cockatoos to the geese, before finally reaching the ducks) that one of the bats had seen a frog on top of the Giant's Teeth. After learning this, they were hoping with all their hearts that Robert was coming back down the same way under the cover of darkness.

So when Robert finally reached the Cave, rather than finding them lying in their favourite spots in the sand as they normally would be at this time of the evening, he found them with their heads close to the gap in the Cave wall where the music flowed through.

"Robert, dear? Are you in there somewhere? Are you hurt?" called Daisy, her voice echoing ever so slightly. "Please say something - we are worried sick for you."

"Robert!" yelled Baz, "Robert! Ro - bert! Can you hear us?"

"Daisy, Baz," said Robert coming up behind them. "It's all right, I'm here."

Well, the two friends looked at each other, and you would not have needed great skills of imagination to see the confusion sweeping through their minds as they both wondered what tricks of sound were making Robert's voice come from behind them.

"Robert, where are you?" called Daisy even more loudly into the hole. "Are you stuck in there? We just heard you loud and clear like the music. Are you still at the top of the Steep Hill?"

"Robert!" yelled Baz. "Do you need me to come and get you? I will, you know."

"I would come too, Robert," added Daisy, quickly, "if I could fit."

"Baz, Daisy, I'm here! Right here, behind you," said Robert louder still, prompting them to spin around with such speed and with such shocked expressions, that it was as if their friend had poked them with sharp sticks rather than merely calling their names.

"Robert! We have been looking for you!" said Daisy, so overwhelmed by her emotions that she could not say another word. Instead, seeking a physical way to express her pained feelings, she bent her head and gently nudged Robert. Due to their size difference, this was as difficult as it sounds, and a great testament to her gentle skills that she did it perfectly.

"Daisy...," said Robert.

"We have been worried sick, Robert," interjected Daisy, "you must tell us if you are ever planning to secretly disappear again."

"Oh, stop being so nice, Daisy!" blurted Baz. "Robert, what were you thinking, going up there without us?! Look, you're covered in scratches. Did you get attacked? Tell me who by and I will see to it."

"Baz! Let him speak. Let him get a word in," interrupted Daisy, who then immediately ignored her own advice. "You must be starving. Are you hungry? Can we get you some food?"

Daisy continued to let out all her care and worry: "Robert, you are going to need a very good night's sleep after this, most probably two..." And Baz interrogated Robert about the details of his long night climbing the Steep Hill: "You were crazy and stupid to do that on your own – you should have asked me. I would have walked through the paddock with you." And in reply, bit by bit, Robert told them everything that had happened.

And as he told them about his long night of difficult and frightening climbing, this is what he heard back from them:

"That was mad, Robert. Imbecilic!" cried Baz, at one point, rapidly snapping his beak open and shut, to fully demonstrate just how much he thought Robert's plan had gone against all sensible action. It was a doubly powerful expression of his feelings, for in general, he was not normally opposed to non-sensible action.

And: "Those... those... bats! What horrible little creatures they are, picking on a small helpless frog," said Daisy, her eyes narrowing, and this time not at all unhappy that she had almost spoken exactly what was on her mind. But then, as though feeling this negative energy needed to be balanced out, she added, "What they really need to do is to change their diet. If only they were to discover just how delicious grass actually is."

But then there was their sad response to the very hardest part of the story, which Robert had been dreading telling them, for he knew the upset it would bring.

"Hennie is gone," he finally was able to get out quietly.

"Oh, that is the worst, just the worst, saddest thing," said Daisy. Her head dropped and tears fell onto the sand. "She was so kind to me when I hurt my nose. And many other times as well."

"And to me too," added Baz, taking a deep breath. "Sometimes she would come to the Pond with Farmer Pat and they would have lovely, sweet seeds. She would always give me a great big handful and stroke my neck. Poor, poor Farmer Pat. He must be dreadfully sad."

And: "There was a music machine? That's where the music was coming from? Now it's broken? Farmer Pat threw it from the Steep Hill?"

For a long while they all sat there together, as they had done many times before on evenings such as these, but this time not saying anything. Just as Robert and Sam had found before them, there was a sense that words were of little use. Instead, they made sure they were close enough to be sure of the presence of each other, and to feel that if they needed it, they could easily lean in a little closer. If their feelings became too strong for them, at least they were near the ones who would be able to bring them the greatest amount of comfort.

Much later, when the moon was high in the sky and it was beginning to get cold, the three friends finally lifted themselves from the floor of the Cave. And as they wandered back along the edge of the Pond, each of them in turn looked up to the top of the Steep Hill, knowing they were not going to hear Farmer Pat or his music. But as they looked up, they still hoped that Farmer Pat might be standing there, looking down at the moon's reflection on the Pond, and that he would see these three animals looking up at him, wanting more than anything for him to know that on this night, he was in their hearts.

When Robert finally got home, he was so exhausted by the day and night just gone, that even though he had more thoughts swirling around his head than ever before, he fell asleep the moment he lay down on his small bed of moss. But this was not a chance for him to escape all these torrid thoughts. No, they merely transformed themselves into troubling dreams which seemed to last the whole night through.

HOW COULD IT BE?

The following morning, just after dawn, Robert lay in his little bed finding himself involved in one of those strange occurrences which happen to us all from time to time, when we are right on the edge of waking up, and we hear, or think we hear, something so curiously different from what we would normally expect to hear, that we wonder if we are awake at all or just dreaming we are awake.

Robert was feeling this sensation as he lay in bed, not ready to open his eyes, but suddenly being forced to after becoming aware that the vague sound he could hear – which he thought was not possible – was Farmer Pat's tractor. Its engine was coughing and spluttering, as it usually did when it stopped at the Pond Paddock's closed gate. Only then did Robert accept that what he was hearing was not a dream, so he leapt out of his bed and hopped up his "staircase" and onto his branch.

But if the sudden, unexpected appearance of Farmer Pat's tractor had generated a moment of hope in his heart, it was gone in a flash when he saw Farmer Pat himself. Even from this distance, Robert could sense something was wrong. "This is not the Farmer Pat I know," he said quietly to himself. "He's not calling out 'hello' to the cows. Or, saying to them, 'anything you need to tell me?' as he normally would. Nor is he stopping to check all the small things."

On another day, all of this could have been explained away as Farmer Pat feeling ill, or being in a hurry to get into the Big Town or to see his friends. This is how the other animals and Robert would have explained it to each other. But Robert now knew far too much to give it any of these explanations.

And as the morning went on, more animals began to notice and feel the change that had taken place in Farmer Pat. On that day, and in the days and weeks that followed, many of the older animals asked each other, "Why is Farmer Pat being like this?" And they would answer, "It's a terrible thing that Farmer Pat has lost Hennie, but it will pass, these things always do." Or, "Do you remember when Mrs Selwyn the cat became very sad after losing her husband and didn't utter a word for weeks? She eventually felt better and began talking again. This will be the same as that. This is how these things go."

There were many variations of these views, but when it was all said and done, they were saying the same thing. If they were boiled down to their common essence, the animals would have been left with one way of behaving around Farmer Pat during this time, which is best captured by the single gentle idea: "There is nothing we animals can do. But that is all right, because if we do nothing, time will heal Farmer Pat. This is how time works."

There was also another view as to how the animals should be acting towards Farmer Pat. It might be best summed up by the phrase, "common sense wisdom", or old, wise ideas passed down from generation to generation such as, "try and touch Farmer Pat's hand when he passes you some food", or, "don't create a big fuss if you think there is not enough seed on a particular day", or, if you were more practically minded, "help Farmer Pat by picking up some hay and putting it into the tractor, because every little bit helps." All these measures, anyone would agree, were deeply well-meaning and from the heart.

But as the weeks after Robert's climb up the Steep Hill turned into months, despite the animals' faith in the broad idea that time and common sense were healers, the sad reality was that neither of them worked. And, as Robert worried to Baz regularly, "Things are just not getting better, Baz. They are getting worse."

"I know, Robert, I know," Baz would answer, his legs beginning to shake a little more each time.

The most obvious way things were getting worse was that the farm was becoming increasingly run down. At first, it was just the little things, changes that only those with the sharpest, most experienced eyes would notice.

But over time these small problems began mixing with one another, and they grew into far larger ones.

One example was that the reeds on the side of the Pond were beginning to grow too long. This was only a small change on the big farm, but after a while, the ever expanding patch of reeds began to clog the water pumps which brought water up to the Stone House.

And without enough water, the grass around the Stone House began to die, which allowed far hardier weeds to take their spot. This in turn made the fence posts more difficult to see, which let the ants and termites eat them without being noticed. The final result was that some of the fences were showing signs of falling over.

These were the fine details Farmer Pat would once have certainly noticed on his morning rounds. And if it were summertime and he could not mend them straight away, he would return in the cool part of the day with the tools and materials to do the necessary repairs. Or if it were winter, he would come back with the tools, and a thermos of tea to keep his hands and insides warm.

But when these small things remained unfixed after many months, the most experienced and wisest animals began to feel that if something was not done soon, the farm would soon become dangerous for the animals. For example, if the fences fell over, some animals – especially the young ones without a good sense of the danger of cars and trucks - might wander into trouble.

With this understanding, the overall mood on the farm finally shifted from "it will eventually get better, just you wait and see", to a much stronger feeling that just waiting and hoping was only going to lead to the lives of the animals becoming far worse.

However, as this new understanding grew, it did not bring a sense of hope, or a call to action. Rather, it carried with it a sense of gloom and helplessness, because to most of them, the question, "What can we do to help Farmer Pat?" was one without a good answer.

Indeed, to most, it felt as if there never could be an answer, as they were "just animals". Not even Robert, who had been thinking longest and hardest about the problem, had been able to arrive at a solution. "How can we help Farmer Pat?" he would ask himself over and over again as he sat on his branch or lay in his bed. Sometimes he did feel that he was sensing a possible way, but no matter how hard he tried, he never seemed to be able to grasp hold of an answer.

A SMALL PIECE
OF HOPE

"What can we do? What can the animals do?" said Baz, when Robert raised the subject as they sat in their favourite spot in the Cave one afternoon. A part of each of them was forever hopeful that somehow, magically, at any moment the music would once again emerge from the rocks.

"I just wish the music machine wasn't broken," said Daisy, a sentence she had said more times in the last months than even her beloved grass story. "I have no doubt that if he could hear the music as he used to, he would feel better. It would be the same if I ever suddenly lost my appetite, God forbid. All you two would have to do would be to find me the magnificent patch of grass, and make me eat it, and I would remember how good the grass tasted and feel hungry again."

77

"Yes," thought Robert, as her words went around his head. "Daisy would remember how wonderful it tasted and would feel hungry again." Then, before stopping and searching his mind to find a more precise way of expressing what his feelings were telling him, he said out loud, "Daisy's right! It's the grass... but it's not literally the grass. If we could get Farmer Pat to hear his music from the music machine again, it might be just as Daisy described – it might help him to feel 'hungry' again."

"But Robert, we can't," replied Daisy, disappointed that Robert's new thoughts, which had begun with such promise, had not led somewhere more satisfactory. "We've talked about this."

"We sure have!" said Baz. "Robert, you told us yourself that the music machine is not just broken, it's smashed."

"And you said we could never reach it," added Daisy.

"And we can't just get another one from the Big Town, can we?" said Baz. "We're just animals."

"Yes..." replied Robert, after letting their comments rest for a moment. "But... but... what if we could make one?"

"Make one?" said Daisy, not even trying to hide her frustration. "Oh, Robert, it is wonderful you would even try. But no animal could make a machine like that. No animal. Only humans can make machines like that."

"Daisy," Robert went on, "I am not saying we should try and make one the same as Farmer Pat's."

"But that is how they are made, my lovely," she replied. "That's the way all his machines are made. You have seen Farmer Pat repair the tractor and the fence and the bridge. It takes all of his tools to do it."

"I know that," replied Robert, "but what if we were to make a music machine from things we know and have?"

"Things we know and have? Like grass? Like hay?"

"No, not like that. I was thinking we make it from us."

"Us? Who, us?" chimed in Baz, confused.

"Us. All the animals," Robert went on. "What if we could make some of the music that used to come from the machine?"

"Oh, Robert, it's a fine idea…" said Daisy, holding off on her next word, only for it to be said by Baz instead.

"But…" began Baz, then stopped, not wanting to hurt Robert's feelings as Daisy had not wanted to before him.

However, Baz's "but" was a very fair "but", for there were so many problems with Robert's idea that Baz could have named ten without even reaching the smaller, hard ones.

"Robert, please, we can't sing like the music machine," said Baz, finally. "We can't even sing like you."

"I've heard you sing," countered Robert, quickly.

Which was true. One day, while paddling on the Pond, Baz had suddenly become so overcome with a memory of Farmer Pat's music, he had burst out singing quite spontaneously. But he had been so embarrassed by the appalled look Mrs Crichett threw him, he immediately tried to cover up everything by furiously coughing. Then he'd called out to her, "I was just trying to warn you, Mrs Crichett, that there was a snake – a snake! But would you believe, just as I was, a large seed blew into my throat. It's out now! Don't worry about me. Worry about the snake!"

"I know she didn't believe me, Robert," Baz said to Robert, mournfully. "Not for a moment. It was humiliating! So you are wrong, my friend. I most definitely cannot sing. I can snore, believe me. I've been told I am an expert. So if snoring is what you need, I'd be all feathers in."

"Baz," replied Robert, "as you have told me many times, you cannot take Mrs Crichett's word…"

"Robert, as it happens, I would very much like to believe in your idea," Baz interrupted, "but – and believe me it hurts me to admit it –the old goose is right about my singing. I cannot sing like you. I am sorry, but really it is impossible."

"I can't either," jumped in Daisy, worried that with Baz speaking so honestly, Robert's task might all fall to her. "You know that, Robert dear. Only you can sing like the music machine. We know this idea has come from deep inside you, but Robert, you must believe us. No matter how much good there is in this idea, it is still going to be impossible."

"Baz, Daisy," Robert said eventually, after thinking about all they had said, "we don't need to sing as well as the music machine. I know that can't be done. But if we could somehow sing nearly like it, just in our own way… I have a strong feeling it might help Farmer Pat to… remember.

Yes, just as you said about the grass, Daisy. Help him to remember something he has forgotten."

"You don't think it would matter if we were terrible?" said Daisy.

"No," replied Robert. "And honestly, I don't think we would be hopeless. I really don't."

"How many animals would we need?" asked Baz, still not at all convinced.

"As many as we could get – that's the key, I think," replied Robert, his understanding of the idea growing with every passing minute. "The more we have, the better it would sound."

"They would be too shy, Robert, too embarrassed," said Daisy. "I just don't think…"

"Oh, there would be a few, Daisy," said Baz, cutting her off. Then he gave her a sharp look just out of Robert's eye line, a look imploring her, "C'mon, Daisy, let's not crush Robert's feelings too much."

"Well, I think there would be many!" said Robert suddenly and loudly. And because the tone was most unlike him, it startled his friends, but also told them that this was more than just an idea to Robert.

"Robert, I am sorry," began Daisy, "we were not meaning to…"

"Daisy," Robert went on passionately, "the animals will want to do it when they hear it will help Farmer Pat. They will want to help him. I know they will. Once they hear that we have an idea."

81

"But how are we going to get everyone to sing, Robert?" said Baz.

This was the very question blaring in Robert's head. And it had another uncomfortable question tucked beside it, which was, "Who on earth is going to listen to a small green tree frog? Is there really a chance that all the big and medium animals on the farm - some of whom I have never met - would listen to me?"

But it was also unavoidably true that he was the only one who knew the music, and could teach it to the others.

"I'm not sure... but I am just going to try to get everyone to sing," he finally got out. "But I will need you both to help me."

No animals in their position - certainly not animals as loyal and kind as Baz and Daisy - were ever going to say no to a small frog who needed their help and physical protection. But more than that drew them to Robert's plan. It was also his passion. When we stumble across such a passion in others, we instinctively know, perhaps by laws that live on the edge of our senses, that this kind of passion is a very wise thing to be a part of, and it is to be held and supported with all our hearts, because it is a rare and beautiful thing.

"Yes, dear, yes..." said Daisy, suddenly feeling inspired, but still not at all sure she could actually help anyone else sing.

"Yes, Robert, you can count on me, too," added Baz.

"Oh, thank you," Robert replied, deeply relieved, because he knew there was not the slightest possibility he could carry out his idea without them. "It would be impossible without your help."

"But how do we do it, Robert?" said Baz, momentarily slipping from the role he was so used to playing, that is, of one not entirely concerned with the reality of things.

"I think the first thing we need to do is to convince everyone we know to come down to the Pond so we can tell them about this idea," answered Robert.

"Yes, that would be a very sensible place to start," said Daisy.

"But how are we going to convince them, Robert?" said Baz. "That's a big problem, a very big one. You know that. I can see it on your face."

"Yes," said Robert, looking away from Baz to hide his worry as much as he could. He did not have a good answer to the question, and he definitely did not want his feelings of uncertainty to spread to his friends any further than they already had.

"Don't worry, Robert," said Daisy, warmly, "we'll work something out."

"Actually... on second thoughts..." said Baz, suddenly standing bolt upright, as though an ant had impatiently wanted him to move out of its way and had delivered a bite in the place it knew would hurt Baz the most, to hurry him along. "Leave it all to me."

"Leave it all to you, Baz?" said Daisy, who was not all adjusted to her dear friend's sudden passion for responsibility.

"I will add it to my news bulletin tomorrow morning. I will tell the whole farm that something incredibly important has happened and that they all need to immediately report to the Pond."

"What happens if they don't believe you?" asked Robert, which was a question that could have been taken the wrong way by Baz, but on this occasion, as the old saying goes, he treated it as water off a duck's back, and grinned at Robert.

"They will, Robert. Just you wait! I'm rather good at this sort of thing."

Then the three friends, sitting as they were on the sandy floor of the Cave, looked at each other and nodded quietly. Although there was now a shared growing determination to see if they could make the plan succeed, they also knew that it would most likely never work. Indeed, it might not last beyond tomorrow morning. But tonight they were going to push these glum thoughts aside, for this was the time to concentrate all their energies and dreams into the task of making another music machine for Farmer Pat.

DOWN TO
THE POND

The following morning, Robert found himself waking up to the unmistakable sound of Baz talking loudly. This was not unusual, of course, but it was unusual that such a large group of animals were talking back to him, just as loudly. This seemed to be positive – indeed, remarkable news. "Brilliant, Baz!" said Robert to himself, leaping up excitedly. "Just brilliant!"

On the Pond surface, however, the news was not nearly as brilliant as Robert was imagining it to be. It was true, Baz had managed to gather many of the farm animals to the Pond's edge, as he had claimed he would be able to. The problem – the very large problem - was that none were there because of Robert's idea.

But these cold facts are not here to paint Baz in a poor light; or, for that matter, to under-appreciate the creativity, skill, bravado, and sacrifice of future reputation that he had needed to waddle and swim around the entire farm, telling every animal he could any number of large and small untruths. He had done it for the simple reason that he knew in his heart that the statement, "Robert wants us all to sing", no matter how it was delivered, would not have budged a single animal – except for some of the birds - from their morning rhythms and routines.

Indeed, would the cows ever believe him again, after he had casually wandered up to them as the sun first popped over the horizon, and told them this?

"I absolutely promise that there is extra hay down at the Pond. I hear your doubt. No, I do not know how it got there. But I did overhear your cow friends talking about it. 'Extraordinary quality!' they were saying between mouthfuls, 'Unusually good for this time of the year!' Yes, I saw it with my own eyes, and heard them with my own ears. If you do not believe me, you will just have to get off the ground and walk to the Pond yourselves, won't you? You should hurry, though. I also heard the other cows whispering, 'Do not tell the other cows about this; let's keep it all for ourselves.'"

And he was certain his relationship with the horse family would be broken until at least this time next year, after telling them:

"Hello! Morning all! I know it's early. Would you believe, I was chatting to one of the snakes last night...

pardon? What's that? Well, there you go, there's something you've learned already and the sun has barely even risen… yes, I do chat to snakes. But what I was trying to say… is they told me they are heading off over the hill this morning to visit relatives. I know! I've never heard of the snakes leaving the property before either. But what an opportunity for you to have a swim in the Pond. Feel how hot it is already!"

But against all the odds, Baz's quick, to-the-point, improvisations worked spectacularly well. Far beyond his wildest expectations, even some of the most difficult and tentative (but now curious) animals had broken their morning routines and headed down to the Pond.

This had happened to such a degree of success that when, moments after hearing Baz's voice, Robert surfaced and clambered onto a lily, he saw the astonishing sight of most of Stone Hill Farm's animals gathered around Daisy, united as never before by their collective displeasure at Baz, who had leapt onto her back for safety. At this moment, Baz spotted Robert, so he stood tall, filled his lungs, and announced at the top of his voice:

"Quiet! Quiet! You have come down here today for many reasons – some of which may or may not be exactly because of the words that I may or may not have said to you earlier. For that, I am sorry. However, there is another very important and significant reason I have brought you all here today. But it has nothing to do with either Daisy or me. We would, however, be grateful, if you would listen to what our dear friend Robert has to say."

The surprisingly serious, earnest tone in which Baz delivered his message caught the gathered group off guard - and if he were honest, Baz himself as well. They all momentarily seemed to forget their angry, annoyed, disappointed and hungry moods and silently stared at Baz, more than a touch puzzled.

"I repeat - this is not about me," Baz went on, sweeping his wing. "It's about Robert." At this, every set of eyes looked to where Baz was pointing, and saw Robert standing at the edge of the Pond.

This was Robert's moment to face the crowd. So he nervously clambered onto Daisy's back, moved past Baz, and stood on her head. Once there, he paused to consider the difficult dilemma of what to say and, equally hard, how to say it. For there was no doubt that what he was going to ask of the gathered group was very strange, and certainly for many, very uncomfortable.

But in the end, Robert decided there was only one option open to him which had any hope of working, and that was to speak from his heart. So he nervously began to tell them his story, mostly about his climbing to the top of the Steep Hill and what he found there.

Now, anyone who has ever told their story to another person, or worse, a large crowd, knows the fear Robert faced as the words began to flow from him. The fear is not so much that people will not listen closely, or that they will start talking to the person standing next to them about what they are having for dinner or something equally bland, gradually becoming louder and louder, which in turn signals others to do the same, until everyone is talking at the top of their voice, and the story has little chance to be heard by anyone at all.

That is terribly rude, and a horrible feeling, but it is not the real fear. The real fear is that the story that is held so close to the heart and gives life a sense of meaning, will be heard but not felt in the same way by the listeners. And that with them turning away from the story, you might question it, or even lose faith in it.

"What if the animals don't care enough about Farmer Pat or his music to try and help him?" Robert thought to himself. But as he spoke, trying to keep the fear to himself, he desperately watched their faces, and soon could see their attention growing, until finally he reached the main point: "We need everyone here to help us help Farmer Pat."

These were the key words. And when he said it, there was not an animal who would have disagreed with the idea of helping Robert, Baz and Daisy. But as we know, this was not the full question. That was: "We need everyone to help us make music, to sing for Farmer Pat. We need to make the music which he has lost, the music that used to come down the Steep Hill at night. But we need all of us to do it. The more of us there are, the more it will help."

As we might expect, after such a powerful, passionate speech, there was a long moment's silence as everyone tried to understand in their own way what this meant to them. Finally, it was Mrs Crichett, who, like Baz - perhaps because water birds often have their feet in cold water and like to keep events moving along - was the one to break the silence.

"Young man, I admire your idea. Really, you are a bold one. I look for that quality in animals so I can show it to my children for them to learn. But I am afraid it is the most preposterous thing I have ever heard. To begin, I am quite tone deaf. Ask anyone. I am not ashamed of it. Not the least. Now, really, if you will excuse me, I wish you the best of luck with your endeavours, but I am unable to dilly-dally a moment longer."

With that she waddled off, calling for her nine little goslings to follow her.

"PLEASE, MRS CRICHETT!"

Mrs Crichett had a very strident, powerful voice on the farm. And, as might be expected when someone of this nature shows leadership on a difficult issue, the smaller, less confident voices tend to follow. No one, in this moment, understood this better than Robert, who realised he had to act fast, because he could see the crowd had begun to look away from him, even those who knew in their hearts they would like to be part of it. So, instinctively, he called out, "Mrs Crichett! Mrs Crichett! Please! Just wait one minute, please. Please!"

Not even someone as perpetually busy and forceful as Mrs Crichett could walk away from a soul like Robert at this point. So she stopped, and without turning her body she craned her long neck back. "Yes, Robert? What is it?

I have told you my opinion. I do not tend to change them once they are made."

"I really need your help, Mrs Crichett," Robert replied, trying his best to hide his deep nervousness. "I know for a fact that everyone here will follow you in what you think and do."

"I'm not sure that is true, Robert," Mrs Crichett replied, even though she was privately very pleased to hear her beliefs about herself being so publicly confirmed.

"It is, Mrs Crichett," Robert replied, "It is... and that is why I need to teach you to how to sing Farmer Pat's music."

"Sing? Me? Farmer Pat's music?"

"Yes. I know I can teach you. You just need to give me a chance."

"Robert. I admire you, young man. I have already made that clear. But I need to remind you of a very well-known fact: geese don't sing. We honk. Nobody wants to hear honking for a moment more than is necessary. Least of all me."

Although no one actually dared say anything, for it seemed important to stay quiet, most of them knew that Mrs Crichett was quite correct.

"Mrs Crichett," Robert persisted, "please, if you could find five more minutes, to give me at least one chance to show you how this might work."

To that, Mrs Crichett didn't say anything. But just as importantly, she didn't say something either. And before she could, Robert surprised even himself by turning to the group and calling out, "Will everyone stay if Mrs Crichett does?"

This was not an easy thing to decide. And in the following moments, each member of the group had their own way of dealing with the tension that this difficult question produced. Some shuffled their feet. Others looked at others from their group as if imploring them to make the decision for the group, only to find sets of eyes looking back with exactly the same question in them.

Some made mumbling noises which had no real meaning, but were preferable to the horrible feeling of saying nothing at all, while one group nervously jerked their eyebrows up and down, as if they were trying to scratch an itch on the inside of their foreheads.

However, what everyone definitely had in common was that they all could think of many reasons not to be there being asked to sing. But because everybody was waiting for everybody else to make the first move, no one actually made the first one. This only increased the tension, especially in Robert, who looked from face to face imploring someone to act boldly and show the others the way.

In the end, the deadlock was broken by one of the sheep, Lucy, who, finding the tension in her body utterly unbearable, became convinced that the only way to relieve it was to nibble a clump of juicy grass at her feet which she had been eyeing off for a full ten minutes.

When she finally gave in to this urge and dropped her head, it seemed to the rest of her flock that she was nodding to Robert that she would stay. The flock, being sheep, saw this as a show of leadership, so naturally followed her lead, and began nodding themselves.

Fortunately for Robert's plan, the sheep were the largest group at the Pond that day, and their sea of nodding heads had the flow-on effect of giving a sense that the majority of animals had made a decision.

Soon every animal was nodding, saying to their neighbour such things as, "Yes, I suppose, if everyone else is staying for a little while longer, we could too." And with that resolved, all eyes turned back to Mrs Crichett.

"Robert," she said in her firmest tone, "you have my attention for five full minutes. Not a minute more, not a minute less." Robert knew this to be true, so he wasted no time, and called out, "Everyone, I have a plan to help Farmer Pat so that he can look after us and the farm properly again. We – all of us - are going to become Farmer Pat's new music machine. We are going to sing together. To prove that we can do this, I am going to get Baz to show you how."

"What?" whispered Baz, caught completely off guard. "Robert... please..."

"Baz, I just want you to sing five notes," Robert whispered back. Then he sang the five slow notes to show him how.

"Just that. All that fuss, for just that?"

"Yes."

"Okay, I will then," said Baz, puffing out his chest. "I will. I will sing those five notes."

But instead of actually doing it, he shuffled his feet while looking down at them.

"Baz," whispered Robert, "please…"

Baz looked hard at Robert, his eyes saying, "This is terribly embarrassing, you know…" before suddenly blurting out the notes, which sent the group into fits of laughter.

However, whether through good skill or good luck, Robert had picked the perfect animal to begin with. For rather than being horrified by this laughter, Baz found the attention quite wonderful. So he didn't stop there, or wait for further instructions from Robert.

Instead, he stood on the tips of his feet and sang the five notes with even greater strength and passion. Indeed, there was no stopping him. It was almost as if his "play button" had become wedged on. And by the time Baz was through his sixth pass, the animals had stopped laughing, and were saying in their heads or muttering under their breath, "That is actually not too bad… I, for one, never thought a duck could sing like that."

After Baz finally finished and was still taking a series of bows, Robert hopped onto the head of Daisy and whispered into her ear, "Okay, Daisy. Are you ready?"

"Me… oh no… that's not possible."

"Daisy, you'll be wonderful, I promise."

"Oh, Robert…"

"For Farmer Pat, Daisy, please."

"Oh, I suppose I can try, Robert. For Farmer Pat, I can try… yes that's something I can do."

"You will be wonderful, Daisy. Just the same notes as Baz. But sing them as low as you can."

As much as Daisy doubted she could sing, Robert was right about the fact that her great big lungs and chest and mouth, were perfect for producing beautiful low sounds. So perfect in fact, that when she had sung the notes and realised exactly how loud and lovely her tone had been, she felt such an acute sense of embarrassment that she immediately lowered her head and stared at the ground.

But instead of the group making fun of her as they had Baz, they were warm and supportive in their praise, especially the other cows, who were filled with the same natural shyness, so were standing up the back. They had received a boost of confidence from watching Daisy succeed, and called out, "Lovely, Daisy! Very brave!"

This open-hearted response from all the animals was the moment in which Robert's confidence in his idea gained a proper power. As he looked around the crowd, he saw that these two simple pieces of singing had changed something in the animals. So he seized the moment.

"Everybody!" he called out. "All those who have low voices like Daisy, I want you to sing like her. Those who feel they have medium voices like Baz, please sing like him. Anyone who has a high voice, you can follow me."

What nobody could have possibly expected or dreamed of even a few minutes before, was that instead of a timid, nervous response, the birds, the crickets, the sheep, the geese, the ducks, the pelicans (who despite their size have very high singing voices) and all the others, sang this first attempt with an enormous, beautiful passion. When they had finished, before they could feel self-conscious, Robert asked them to do it again. Then again.

After they had finished, they all looked at each other with a mixture of astonishment and pride and thrill, before erupting into the loudest conversation anyone had ever heard at Stone Hill Farm. Some were talking with their group of similar voices about how good they had sounded. Others were debating which of the groups was the best.

There was, however, universal agreement that, despite all the reservations and worries (except, of course, from the birds, to whom singing was the most natural thing in the world) doing the actual singing had been a wonderful thing. It had given them all a sense – one that animals such as Robert are naturally born with - that music could make you feel in ways that other things could not.

"If everyone could... I'm sorry, if we could just have a moment... everybody!" called Robert, who was not only trying to speak above the noise and keep the group focused on the task at hand, but also mindful that he did not want to break the spell of the music. "First... excuse me... I would just like to say how marvellous it was to hear all your voices. But now I would like you to do it again."

As anyone who has ever been a member of a music group or tried to organise a group of people to do something new together will know, the first performance, despite all its passion, was far from perfect. But in amongst the first passes, Robert had also heard a moment or two where the voices had combined in a way that told him that the music machine idea had every chance of working.

Of course, the second attempt at singing was, in most parts, as jumbled and fumbled as the first. But by the fifteenth try, they were starting to get the hang of singing together. And by the thirtieth try, there was the faintest sense that you could hear the music from the music machine.

After many more times through, Robert finally dropped his arms, and the animals stopped singing.

For a moment, there was total silence. The five beautiful repeating notes they had been singing, which Robert had first learned from Farmer Pat and then later heard in the Cave, had deeply touched them all.

The spell was finally broken by Baz, who jumped onto Daisy's head again and called out, "All in favour of Robert's plan, raise your wings!"

One by one the animals raised their wings, paws, hoofs, claws, or, in the case of Claude the Green Tree Snake, sat up straighter. This was the moment when Robert's plan to replace the broken music machine with the farm animals began in earnest.

LEARNING TO SING

If a boy or a girl had been standing on top of the Steep Hill the following evening, they would have seen something that caused them to rub their eyes, then pinch their cheeks, and then even pinch the cheeks of their brother or sister, to check if indeed they were awake.

What they would have been seeing down below, just after the sun's last rays dropped over the hill for the night, was all of Stone Hill Farm's animals walking from their homes and favourite spots towards the edge of the Pond.

Now, if these children were relatively inexperienced in the world of farm animals – perhaps only occasionally visiting their grandparents' farm, for example - they might for a moment have thought that because the animals all looked so natural, relaxed and unhurried, this was a normal, albeit strange, evening happening on this farm.

But then, after staring at this scene for a moment or two longer, they would have certainly been puzzled and begun to ask each other, "Hold on, have you ever read about, or heard of, ducks going near tree snakes?" Or, "I am quite certain that crickets and birds usually only meet when birds are ready for dinner. But here they all are, gathered together?"

If they had kept watching, they would have been even more astonished when they saw that all these animals, big and small, were forming a tight semi-circle in front of a large dairy cow.

"We definitely need to have a closer look at this," the sister might have said to the brother. "Let's get Great-Grandfather's old binoculars."

And when the children had scampered to the barn and fetched them, and had looked down upon the animals in close-up, their confusion would only have grown, because it would have seemed to them that the reason the animals were gathered in front of the large cow's head, was because there was a small green frog standing on top of it.

Now, if they had kept staring - and it is hard to imagine why they would not want to – nothing would have become clearer at all when they also occasionally saw a duck jumping on and off the big cow's back, appearing to talk to the crowd of animals.

And although they couldn't hear the animals because they were a long way away, and their voices didn't have the same loudness as a music machine, in the end they would have been left with only one reasonable conclusion as to what they were seeing. "That's very, very odd. It looks like the animals are singing together."

This is how it would have looked from high up on the Steep Hill - like some kind of event that was beyond understanding when viewed from up so high. But on the ground, from the point of view of Robert standing atop Daisy's head, it was all beginning to make particularly good sense.

Not that it had felt that way all week for Robert. At times, after they had gathered to practise, Robert had swum home with his head filled with doubt and worry as to whether they could ever possibly sing as well as the music machine. But whenever he began to feel it was beyond the reach of them, he would remember the three things driving him forward, and gain fresh courage from them.

The first was that the singing was only a backup plan. Every morning he still woke with the hope that near sunset, the old music would drift down from the top of the mountain as it always had, because Farmer Pat had got his music machine working again.

The second was the actual piece of music they were learning. Robert had no name for it, but it was the piece Farmer Pat had played many times, and had whistled down by the Pond. And even though they were only singing a very small piece of it – just a large handful of beautiful notes - there was something about it that gave him a deep sense of comfort. No matter how worried or nervous he felt, when he heard the animals singing this piece of music, his hope and confidence was restored.

The third was the animals themselves. They too were falling in love with what they were doing and the music they were singing - even those having difficulty remembering their parts or staying in tune, or who were still a little uncomfortable being around other animals that nature told them it would be wiser to keep well away from.

But by the end of the week, when the mistakes were becoming fewer and further between, and the crickets at last seemed to understand it was all right for them to sing a little quieter, and the sheep learned that by swaying their necks they could stay in time with Robert, and the geese finally accepted that their honking fitted into the overall sound very well, he knew it was time for them to perform it for Farmer Pat.

"Everyone, I think it's time we sang for Farmer Pat," Robert announced nervously at the next evening's gathering, and all doubts as to whether they thought they were ready disappeared as his words set off a firecracker of excitement.

"So tonight, go to bed early," called Baz, revelling in his official job as Robert's organiser, after all these years of only having his volunteer job. "We need everyone hidden down by the Pond by the time Farmer Pat drives down here on his tractor in the morning."

FARMER PAT'S TRACTOR

The following morning, Robert, though nervous, had slept well, and was awake early having his breakfast, when he was startled by the muffled sound of the tractor coming down the driveway at an earlier time than normal. "This is it!" he told himself, diving into the water, full of energy, ready to gather the animals who, he was sure, would be already hurrying to the Pond themselves anyway.

But as Robert's head surfaced, he quickly realised that the engine sound was not from the tractor, but from Farmer Pat's truck. "Which is not necessarily bad news," he told himself as he swam to the shore. For he remembered a time when the blue tractor had broken down near the back track's old fence and Farmer Pat had come down to the Pond in the truck to carry out his morning routines.

But still, to ease his mind, he quickly hopped out of the Pond, then without even thinking about crows, onto the same small mound where he had previously searched the upper paddock for Baz and Daisy when they had been looking for Daisy's grass. Once there, he easily located the truck moving slowly along the driveway, then watched intently as it approached the turnoff to the Pond Paddock track.

But to his intense disappointment, it did not turn right. Instead, as Robert watched, it drove straight past the turnoff and continued along the driveway until it was through the big wooden front gates. "We're not going to be singing today," Robert thought to himself, "but we'll be even better tomorrow after another practice."

But these more positive thoughts were interrupted when Robert turned to go home and, out of the corner of his eye, saw Farmer Pat stop the truck. Then, a few moments later, he got out, walked back to the gates and began to close them. This was something Robert had never seen him do before, and it sent a cold shock through him.

But if this deeply uncomfortable, cold feeling had something slightly uncertain about it which left room for hope that Farmer Pat's unusual actions might not be anything to worry about, it was gone in a heartbeat when he saw Sam burst through the long grass lining the fence at the top the Pond Paddock. "Oh no, something bad has happened," Robert thought to himself, his stomach beginning to feel utterly horrible.

"Sam! Sam!" he called out, not caring that he was bringing attention to himself while still so vulnerable out in the open. "I'm over here!"

Just a few moments later, an out-of-breath Sam reached Robert. When Robert saw the same deep worry on Sam's face that he had previously seen the morning atop the Steep Hill, and realised she couldn't speak at first because her throat was so choked up, he had a strong sense of what she was going to tell him.

Finally, Sam got out the words, "Robert, Farmer Pat is leaving the farm. I think he might be leaving forever." And even though a part of Robert was prepared for these words, another part of him - the innermost part of every creature which can never be prepared for such things - took the full blow of this terrible news.

WHAT SAM
HAD SEEN

Standing there with Robert on the small mound, Sam was feeling as horrible as Robert was. But she had one small consolation that Robert did not, which was that she'd had some time to become used to the news. For over the previous week she had been watching closely and listening with great concentration as a series of events took place at Stone Hill Farm. She did not fully understand them, but they had each left her with a nasty, uneasy feeling.

"How can you be sure, Sam?" said Robert, devastated and barely able to speak.

"All week there have been strange people looking around the house and barn, Robert. When I barked at them, Farmer Pat got cross and tied me up at my kennel. He never used to do that."

"No, he would never have done that," replied Robert quietly.

"Then this morning, he packed his truck with many things from inside the house. I've never seen him do that before either."

"What sort of things, Sam?"

"They were not things for working on the farm. They were bags and boxes. But after he had put them in, there was no room for me. And there is always room for me when he goes in the truck, Robert."

"Yes… yes…" replied Robert, doing his best to try and make sense of all he was hearing. "You always go with him."

"Then he walked me to the neighbours, who tied me up. That has never happened before either, Robert. And when Farmer Pat was leaving, he gave me a very long hug and pat. This was when I knew something was wrong, very wrong."

"Yes, very wrong, Sam."

"So when Farmer Pat walked away, all I could do was to start pulling on my lead as hard as I could. The neighbour told me to stop but I wouldn't, Robert. I just kept pulling with all my might until my collar broke."

✳

From the time Sam first explained it to Robert, it took only a few more minutes for the whole farm to hear the news. And as the full truth sunk in, the shocked and frightened animals kept to their own small groups, occasionally shaking their heads in disbelief, or climbing to high parts of the paddocks hoping to catch a glimpse of something which might, against all the odds, show them that Sam had somehow got the story wrong. Or even better, that the big wooden gates would suddenly swing open again and Farmer Pat would drive through.

✳

"We will just have to go and get Farmer Pat back," said Robert quietly, in answer to Baz's question about whether there was anything they could do.

"But Robert, we don't know where he is," said Sam.

"I know, Sam," answered Robert, "but we have to look - we have to."

"But how would we find him?" asked Baz.

"He could be anywhere, Robert," added Daisy.

"I don't know," replied Robert. "All I know is that we need to try. At least we need to do that. Do you all agree with me?"

"Robert," replied Daisy, gently, "we're just animals. I'm just a big cow. And Sam has got her sore legs. Baz can't even fly."

Then she stopped speaking and let a great sigh carry her deepest feelings to the surface. "Sometimes, Robert... sometimes... you have to accept the end of things. I'm so sorry. You have done so much."

"It is not the end of things," Robert said quietly as much to himself as to the others, after a moment when no one was at all sure who was going to say the next word. "This is not the end of things, I promise you; and I will show you."

With that, he jumped from the log he was sitting on, and began hopping up the Pond Paddock path.

"Robert! Where are you going?" called Baz, alarmed.

"To the Big Town," Robert called back. "To find Farmer Pat and bring him back."

"But he might not even be there, Robert!" called Daisy.

"We don't know that," Robert called back. "But I have to try."

"Robert!" yelled Sam, sternly, beginning to get very angry at the whole situation. "You can't just hop down the road! You'll get eaten by the crows. Or by something else. You need to wait until night time, at the very least."

"There's not enough time," called Robert, his voice already becoming hard to hear.

As Robert hopped away, Baz, Sam and Daisy looked at each other without saying anything. But if one of them had said, "I have the most horrible sick feeling in my stomach," the other two would have quickly agreed. For none wanted to leave Stone Hill Farm to travel to the Big Town. They were all wise and experienced enough to know that without Farmer Pat's protection, it was a journey filled with many risks.

But what could they do when their friend, who was just a small frog - much smaller than each of them - was willing to go there on his own?

As they watched him getting smaller and smaller, the three friends were feeling deeply uncertain; but without saying anything, they understood that they were each going to have to face the same very difficult decision that every human or animal who has ever departed on a journey to somewhere unknown has had to face. Do I stay or do I go?

CATCHING UP
TO ROBERT

Catching up to Robert did not take long. For not only was each of their steps worth more than his, but also, Robert was not hopping as fast as he could have been.

From the first hop, he had been wishing with every part of his body that his friends would be unable to see or guess just how scared he was. With every hop he took, he was not at all sure another was possible without looking back to see if they were coming after him. His deepest worry was that they would believe he felt brave enough to hop along the road by himself all the way into the Big Town.

When they reached him, Sam took charge.

"Robert," she said, stopping in front of him, "we are going to come with you, but I insist that we wait until night-time before we take another step. It's far too dangerous for us all to go now."

"Sam, I'm sorry," replied Robert, hopping past her, "but we cannot waste a single minute, we need to keep…"

"Robert," she interrupted, positioning herself in front of him again, "a cow wandering the roads would be noticed very quickly by humans, and caught and brought back to the farm."

"Maybe I should stay behind then?" offered Daisy.

"That's not at all what I meant, Daisy," replied Sam. "If we are going to succeed, we are going to need everyone. But we must wait until it is dark."

Even for someone as determined as Robert, it was hard to argue with Sam's wisdom. So after a few slower hops, he was finally convinced to stop and wait until sunset.

At that time of the year, deep into autumn and on the cusp of winter, this meant the friends did not have to wait long before the sun disappeared behind the mountains. But even after it was gone, they waited until the stars became visible before feeling it was safe to once more start their journey.

When they did, to begin with, they all started walking, waddling and hopping at their own pace. But when they began to become separated, Sam, who was out front, stopped and turned to the others. "Robert," she called, "we have no hope of reaching the Big Town tonight at the rate we are going."

"Sam, just because I can't fly, it doesn't mean that I can't walk quickly," answered Baz proudly, immediately waddling more quickly, until he was past Sam. "But I am sure Robert can do with some help."

This was true, for while hopping is good for short walks and long jumps, it is very hard to do for lengthy periods of time, as Robert had found when he climbed the Steep Hill. So while he did not want to show this weakness to his friends for fear that they might decide not to go into the Big Town, he was very relieved and grateful when Daisy called, "Sam is right. Hop on my back, dear; I will hardly know you are there."

After another few hundred metres down the road, when Baz's small waddling legs became increasingly tired, he too scrambled onto Daisy's back, muttering under his breath that he had stood on a sharp stone and he was only going to stay here for a short while, plus Robert looked like he needed some company. And Daisy was so strong that she hardly noticed that he was there either.

✻

What a strange sight it would have been to anyone who chanced to see the four friends walking along the road that night. A dog leading a large dairy cow, with a duck and a small frog riding on her back. All of them were largely silent, apart from the odd word to help lift the spirits of anyone who was struggling; or to help with practical things, such as Sam calling, "watch out for the deep puddle," or Baz saying, "I am really starting to get the feeling that we can find Farmer Pat, I can truly feel it in my feathers." Even though they all knew that when Baz said things like this it usually meant he was feeling the opposite inside himself, there was still something comforting and hopeful in hearing him say it out loud.

The exchanges during these hours were kept brief and whispered because they had enough animal wisdom to know that even though it was dark, if someone heard an unfamiliar dog barking or a stray cow mooing, that person might very well stop what they were doing and pull back their curtains and peer outside.

And our friends knew, with an absolute certainty, that if someone did this, they would be seen and caught, and everything would be over.

So they travelled silently and carefully along the darkest parts of the road, worried that at any moment they would be noticed, until they reached the wide bitumen road which marked the edge of the Big Town.

Here they found a thin clump of bushes to hide in, which had just enough of a cleared area within its middle for them to sit comfortably together, but also gave a good view of the Big Town's streets.

"Look how light the Big Town is," said Baz. "How are we going to walk around the streets with them all lit up like that?"

"And there are people driving in their cars," added Daisy, feeling deeply unsettled. "They should all be home looking after their children."

"I suppose everyone else heard the dog barking, too?" said Baz, glumly. "There are going to be many, many dogs in a place like this."

"Yes, there will be. Yes... but we will still find a way," said Robert, working hard to stop himself from saying out loud the worried thoughts circling through his mind. "Sam, what do you think?"

"I think it is best if I go ahead alone," responded Sam, after a moment, "to see what I can find."

"Oh, really, Sam?" said Daisy. "Do you think that's a good idea? It looks like such a terribly dangerous place. You said yourself we should all work together."

"I agree with Daisy," added Robert, quickly. "Don't you think the best chance we have is if we all stay together?"

"But I will fit in the best," replied Sam. "It would not be unusual to see a dog walking the streets. You three might all be caught quickly, or worse."

"Sam is right, but I still don't understand how we are going to find Farmer Pat," said Baz, pointing at the town, then standing up and stretching his neck, as if to make it absolutely clear that he was making a very important point. "Without that, nothing else can happen. Look at the size of the town. No matter who goes, we are still not going to be able to find Farmer Pat here. It is going to be impossible."

"I think I have an idea how to find Farmer Pat," replied Sam, with a surprising calmness.

"You do?" said Baz, taken aback.

"Yes… maybe…" answered Sam. "I'm not sure if it will work. I don't know. I can't be certain. But for it to work, I will definitely need to go ahead alone."

"Why? What is the plan?" asked Robert.

"I will tell you when I get back," replied Sam, quickly looking away from them, giving the impression she was hiding something.

"Do you really have a plan, dear Sam?" asked Daisy, kindly. "You're not just going ahead to protect us, are you? Please don't do that."

"Yes, I really do," replied Sam, "although, as I have said, the only way it will work is if I go alone. But you must promise me that you will stay hidden in the trees until I come back. It's not a very good hiding spot. You could easily be discovered here, too."

"We won't move," said Robert.

"Not even to stretch my wings, Sam. I will just sit here," added Baz.

"Sam, are you sure?" said Robert, "We will come with you if you ask us to. We really will. Just as you all have come with me."

"Robert, I'm certain," she replied, moving to the edge of the small clearing. "But if something happens and I don't come back, promise me you will wait until it's dark again before you walk home. Even if you have to wait a whole day."

"Yes," said Robert, hoping with all his heart that it would never come to that.

"Don't worry, you'll come back," added Baz quickly. Then, as if to make sure of it within himself, he repeated his sense of conviction to the others. "Sam will come back. I guarantee it."

"Good luck, dear," called Daisy, quietly.

"Yes, good luck, Sam," added Robert.

But by then Sam had pushed through to the other side of the bushes. And as they watched her hurry down the road, the three remaining friends were hit with an equal sense of powerlessness that there was nothing they could do now but sit and wait until she got back, which was a feeling with a very bitter taste to it.

GOING AHEAD
ON HER OWN

Despite Daisy's doubts, Sam did have a plan. But she didn't want to share the details of it with her friends unless she absolutely had to, because it would have meant revealing to them something dogs try to keep a secret amongst themselves.

The secret is this: when we listen to dogs barking at their front fences, or in their back gardens, generally the topics they are barking about fall into three categories. The first one is trespassing: "This is my house, stranger! Stay away!"

The second topic is empty stomachs: "Does anyone fully understand how hungry I am?" And the third - the worst - is when boredom sets in when their owner is away at work or school: "When is someone coming home? I need someone to throw a ball to me!"

If you were to ask any reasonable dog, they would certainly agree that most of the time this is what dogs are barking about.

Occasionally, however, the barking is about something else. And the way to recognise it is when the barking moves in a pattern. That is, the barking begins at one home, but rather than stopping there, or getting a single response or two from neighbouring dogs, who are just as lonely, hungry or worried as they are, it spreads across a much wider area, in every direction. It is the same as what happens when a stone drops into a pond and causes water to ripple in every direction.

In all cases, this "barking ripple" happens for a single reason. It starts when one dog suddenly understands that an unfamiliar dog who has wandered into its territory is not there to steal its food, does not want to take over its house, or is just being bossy, but rather, it is in need of some "true help."

And if there is one issue in the world of dogs which always receives "some true help" - touching a dog's heart more than any other reason and lighting up the dog network in its full intensity - it is when one dog tells another, "I have lost my family, can you please help me find them." Every puppy learns from their mother and father about how to get true help from other dogs.

So when Sam turned off the bitumen road into a smaller house-lined street, she was in search of true help.

But she also knew that before she could receive it, she would have to endure the loud aggressive barking that would soon be heading in her direction from the first dog she passed.

She did not have to wait long. For only three houses down the street, she heard the distinctive clacking sound of dog claws scrambling up from a wooden front porch, then racing down the front steps, up to the fence. "This is my house!" the dog barked at the top of its lungs. "This is my house! Go away, go away!"

Under normal circumstances, Sam would have done exactly as this big dog was asking her to do. But on this occasion, to make sure the dog understood she was not here for unfriendly reasons, she took a few steps backward, dropped down, and waited for it to realise she was instead seeking some true help.

✳

Back at the hiding place, Robert, Baz and Daisy had heard the barking as well.

"Sam hasn't even got past the first few streets," said Baz, grimly.

"It sounds like a large dog, too," added Daisy. "I do hope she's safe and hasn't been attacked. That would be the most terrible thing imaginable."

"She can look after herself, Daisy," said Robert, firmly. "I've seen that before. She's very strong and brave."

"But Robert, even if that is so, you are not understanding something," said Baz, sadly. "Whatever Sam's plan was, it hasn't worked. She's been discovered."

"Maybe we should have gone with her after all," added Daisy, feeling deeply annoyed with herself. "I should have been more..."

"Pushy," said Baz, finishing Daisy's sentence with the correct word, which he knew Daisy would never have used herself. "Me too, Daisy! I should have been pushier as well."

"I'm not giving up yet," replied Robert, even though the look in his eyes told the other two that he was beginning to feel the brave quest to find Farmer Pat had just ended.

"Then what do you think we should do, Robert?" asked Daisy.

But before Robert could answer with the truth - that he didn't have an answer - the dog stopped barking.

"It's stopped," said Robert, almost not believing his ears.

"I think it has," added Daisy.

"Maybe Sam found a way to get past it?" said Baz.

"Yes, maybe, Baz," said Daisy, with just a pinch of hope in her voice.

"But what were you going to say, Robert?" said Baz. "I could see on your face you were worried. That's not good at all. I am beginning to get a very bad feeling about this trip. All of it."

"Baz, please..." started Daisy, "we need to stay positive."

But before Baz could expand on his bad feelings, they were confirmed and strengthened when the dog started barking again; only this time it was even louder and more forceful.

"Oh, no…" said Daisy.

Then even worse news reached the ears of the three friends. For this dog's barking set off a chain of other dogs, to the point where it soon seemed that every dog in the town was barking at the top of their lungs.

"Robert!" said Daisy, in the sternest voice she was capable of. "What hope is there?"

"No hope… is the answer to that very good question," said Baz, waddling around the small space trying to release some of the terrible tension taking over his body. "There is no hope."

"All we can do now is wait for Sam," said Robert, quietly. "I am sure she'll be back in a minute. She cannot be far away."

Although the others did not have the same faith as Robert – not in the slightest – the truth was there was nothing left to them but to wait. So for the next five minutes they remained quiet, just sitting, hoping that against the odds Sam was somehow all right.

But when the five minutes turned into ten, each privately began to accept the worst possibility, that Sam had been hurt by another dog or caught by a human. And as these thoughts wove their way through Robert's mind, he began to feel the most terrible burden crush down upon him, for there was no escaping the fact that it was his plan - one he had insisted his friends carry out with him - and that it had turned out in such a terrible way.

"I think we should go and try to find Sam," Robert finally said, unable to bear the situation a moment longer.

"Yes... I think we should..." replied Daisy, with a great fear in her voice, for she was horribly scared of the prospect of running into a pack of the dogs. "Yes, we must. And go home. We have done what we can now."

"But Sam told us..." Baz interjected, "we were not to leave here and go into the Big Town."

"I know, Baz," replied Robert, "but I don't think even she knew how hard it might be. I think we should at least see what is on the other side of the black road. Look, see those trees over there? We could hide in them as a start."

"Yes, let's do that, but I will go first," said Daisy, "and if someone sees us, or attacks us, you are to both jump onto my back immediately. Am I clear?"

"Yes, Daisy, thank you," replied Robert.

"Okay, so we're going into town," said Baz, his legs trembling; but he was feeling relieved that Daisy was taking over for a moment. "Anything is better than just sitting here. I think we all agree with that!"

With this rough plan to hurry across the road to the next set of trees agreed upon, Daisy began pushing into the bushes directly in front of them, to create a way through them for the others. But as she began to do this, there was a sudden loud rustling noise on the other side of them.

"Hurry! There's something coming. Get onto my back! Make yourselves safe," implored Daisy. She turned around and quickly lowered her head, whispering, "Jump up, you two! Get up!"

But just as Robert and Baz were scrambling onto Daisy's back, Robert's sharp eyes saw who was making their way through the trees.

"It's Sam!" he cried out, joyfully. "It's Sam."

"Sam's back!" yelled out Baz, not caring that he might be heard.

"Sam, we're just here, dear," called Daisy, "just on the other side of the bushes."

"I can see you now," Sam called back. "I'm almost there."

"Oh, thank goodness you're safe, dear," said Daisy, leaning down and snuffling Sam's back with her nose, as she pushed through the last of the foliage into their hiding place.

"But what happened, Sam?" asked Baz impatiently, as he too leaned into Sam. "All that barking! We thought you had been captured or attacked."

But before the out-of-breath Sam could answer Baz's question, Robert spoke first.

"I-I-I... just feel so terrible that Sam was almost attacked by other dogs. It was my idea to come all this way to find Farmer Pat. You are true and wonderful friends to have come with me. I so wish we could have found Farmer Pat, but that is not going to be possible. So now that we are safely back together, we need to hurry home before the sun rises."

127

"Robert, you don't understand," replied Sam, confused. "We can't go back now."

"Oh, Sam… but we can, we have to," said Daisy.

"But we can't," Sam went on. "I know where Farmer Pat is."

"What? You do?" asked Baz, deeply perplexed.

"How…?" added Robert, doubtfully.

"But all those dogs were barking at you," said Daisy.

"Then he can only be nearby," said Robert, gathering his senses, and also feeling a small bit of hope after hearing this remarkable piece of news. "And he can only be in one of these streets, just over there. Did you see his truck?"

"No, Robert, he's not nearby," replied Sam, muddling his friends' thoughts again. "I wish I had better news, but he's not close at all. The dogs told me Farmer Pat is on the other side of town."

"The other side of town?" said Robert, his heart sinking.

"How do you know that?" asked Daisy.

"I'm so confused," said Baz. "I'm not the only one – I can't be."

❋

The others finally believed what Sam was saying. It took many strong, convincing words, especially when Sam added another piece of barely believable good news - that all the dogs of the town had agreed to give them a free, quiet passage through the town. And it brought to them all the beautiful feeling of letting themselves believe that their quest to bring Farmer Pat home was again possible. It was the most wonderful, treasured thought, coming as it did so soon after they had all believed that they'd lost him forever.

A HIDING SPOT

If anyone in the Big Town had been paying attention that night, wondering why the dogs had suddenly gone so quiet after being so noisy only a few minutes earlier, and had gone to check for themselves, they would have found the dogs were not silent at all, but were whispering to one another.

"Sam, make sure you and your friends take the turn at the next big tree. Big Louie will guide you from there." And, "Be careful, Sam, according to Millie there are some humans sitting out the front of a house up on the next street, go down the bumpy lane instead."

This quiet barking went on for many remarkable minutes, carefully guiding the four grateful friends along the dark back streets of the Big Town (always with a far scarier sense that someone would find them or chase them away, or call the police) until they eventually reached their destination.

This was a long, wide street, lined on each side with exceptionally tall, thick-branched pine trees, giving the four friends the feeling that they were walking along a high-walled street. But if this "wall" brought with it a sense of foreboding or entrapment, it evaporated halfway along, when they spotted in the distance Farmer Pat's truck parked outside a large, older building. If they had been able to read, they would have seen a sign, out the front, which said, "No Vacancy".

"There he is!" shouted Baz, barely believing his eyes.

"He's really still here, as the dogs promised," replied Robert, his voice barely above a whisper.

"Oh, thank goodness for that," added Daisy, bursting into tears. "Thank goodness for that! There he is. He hasn't gone yet. Can you believe it? Farmer Pat is really still here." This was such a powerful burst of emotion that none of the others responded further, for Daisy's words and tears had said everything they had been hoping and hiding in their hearts for the entire walk.

Just a few moments later, the four friends were crouched in a little nook, tucked behind a small wall a short distance from the window near where Farmer Pat's truck was parked.

"Does anyone have any idea what we should do next?" asked Baz.

"I have one," answered Sam, "at least, the start of one."

"I don't have a single one," said Daisy. "Not even a beginning – I am still feeling too happy to think."

"Well, I have a sense that if Farmer Pat were to find Daisy here, he would have to take her home," Sam continued.

"Yes, he wouldn't just leave her here, would he?" said Baz, understanding Sam's point.

"I cannot believe he has been changed so much by what has happened that he would do that," responded Daisy softly.

"Yes. If Farmer Pat discovers Daisy, he will have to take her home," added Robert, looking hard at the window. "Which means, Daisy, we need Farmer Pat to see you. As soon as possible."

"I'd like to see him, too, Robert, as soon as possible," smiled Daisy, her heart swelling at the thought of it.

"I wonder..." Robert went on, not at all sure as to how they were going to get Farmer Pat to see Daisy without them all being discovered by someone else. "Do you think we should just creep up to the window and have a look?"

"What happens if he is not in there?" asked Daisy.

"And someone else is?" said Baz, feeling as though there was never going to be a moment where a part of the plan would come easily. "We might get caught."

"I think we just have to take the chance," said Robert. "I keep having a bad feeling that if we don't hurry, Farmer Pat might suddenly drive away and be gone forever."

"Yes, we should hurry," added Sam.

With that, knowing he had his friends' support, Robert jumped onto a nearby branch, then onto Daisy's back, before hopping up to her head. Just a few moments later, he was being raised to the height of Farmer Pat's window.

"What can you see?" called Baz, not even waiting until Robert was actually leaning against the glass.

"Robert, tell us. What you can see?" pressed Daisy, more urgently. "We need to know."

"Robert, is he there?" asked Sam, a terrible tension in her voice. "Somebody is sure to come past at any moment. Our luck will run out at some point."

Here was the truth of what Robert saw and felt when he first looked through the window, and why it took a few extra moments to respond to his waiting friends.

What he saw was Farmer Pat sitting by himself at a small dinner table, deep in thought. For an animal like Robert, who was so open to the feelings of others, it was not hard to see that here was someone who was in a great deal of pain. Someone who was most probably considering the truth of the fact that he had just left behind a lifetime of memories, but memories he just could no longer face daily on his own. Oh, how Robert felt a moment of the deepest connection with the sadness in Farmer Pat. Which, in turn, had the effect of making his desire to help him even more intense.

"Farmer Pat is in there. Just by himself," said Robert, finally. "He looks terribly sad and lonely. We were right to come."

"Should we just try tapping on the glass," said Sam, "to show him that we are here?"

"Yes. But there's a problem," replied Robert.

"Oh, there's always a problem!" said Baz. "Never have there ever been so many problems!"

"Baz, it's nothing serious," Robert replied quickly. "It's just that my hands are too soft to make a noise on the glass. Baz, you will have to do it with your beak."

"Me?" replied Baz. "Is that such a good idea? I don't always get things right."

"You're the best idea we have, dear. It's up to you," said Daisy soothingly, lowering her head to make it easier for Robert to hop off, and for Baz to climb on.

"Do I really need to?" Baz asked.

"Yes, you do! Now get on quickly," Daisy said, in no mood for any of Baz's nonsense. "Onto my head."

A few short seconds later, after regaining his composure, Baz whispered down, as he rose on Daisy's head, "Up... up... up... Stop! I am at the perfect tapping height," he said, peering into the window. "Shall I tap now?"

"Yes!" replied Robert and Sam together.

"All right, I will," Baz replied, giving the window three quick taps, then on instinct dropping down out of sight.

"Did Farmer Pat hear the taps?" asked Robert urgently.

"I can't be certain," replied Baz, looking down at Robert.

"You can't be certain?" said Daisy, unable to see what was going on, and exasperated by her friend's profound inability to make good decisions under pressure.

"Tap the glass again, then, Baz," said Sam, "to be sure of it."

"Do you think it's a good idea?" replied Baz.

"Yes!" said Daisy.

"And hurry!" added Robert, who was getting more awful feelings that they were going to be caught at any second.

"Okay! I'll do it then," responded Baz, stretching up once again to his full height. But as he reached it, he saw that Farmer Pat was approaching the window.

"He's nearly at the window," Baz whispered, immediately dropping down again. "Now what do we do?"

"Hide! Everybody hide!" replied Robert, urgently. "Except you, Daisy. You need to be found."

"Sam! Don't move," Baz called out as he jumped from Daisy's back onto Sam's, then onto the ground, before joining Robert and Sam as they scrambled back behind the wall.

Once safely hidden, they turned back just as Farmer Pat opened the window and looked up into the nearby tree branches.

"Look down!" said Baz, under his breath.

"Yes, look down, Farmer Pat," added Robert.

Then, as though Farmer Pat sensed the needs of his hidden animals, he looked down.

"He heard us!" said Baz.

"Shhh…" replied Robert, "I think he's about to say something."

"Daisy?" Farmer Pat said, after getting over his astonishment at seeing one of his cows standing below his window. "Daisy," he repeated, "is that really you?" Then, after leaning a little further out the window and checking the green tag in her ear, which said "Daisy, Stone Hill Farm", he continued, "It is you, girl. What... how... on earth have you found me here? Sometimes I wonder about you animals, I really do." Then, after stroking her head for a moment, he added, "Now, don't move, girl. No more wandering. I'm going to come to you this time."

Seconds later, Farmer Pat hurried out the motel's front door, plucked a good handful of grass from the edge of the lawn, and slowly approached Daisy. But what Farmer Pat did not know was that he did not need the grass or the soothing words to stop Daisy running away. For she was desperate to see him, and so she hurried over and buried her head into his chest, looking for nothing more than the daily head scratch she had been receiving from Farmer Pat her whole life.

"Hello, Daisy, girl," said Farmer Pat, his voice wavering, while giving her head a thorough scratch and her neck some warm, firm pats. "You could have been run over, do you know that? Wandering the roads all on your own. I would never have forgiven myself if that had happened. Now, we need to get you back home and check the gate before I catch my plane first thing tomorrow."

He then led her to his truck, retrieved some old rope, and looped it around her neck before tying the other end to a branch. "Don't worry, Daisy, I won't be too long. I'll be back before you know it." With that, he hopped into his truck and drove away.

"Now what do we do?" said Baz, as they watched the truck drive away.

"We wait for him to come back," answered Robert.

"Yes, all we can do is hide, and hope he will be back," said Sam, sighing deeply then dropping heavily to the ground.

"If he doesn't, the plan is over," added Baz, grimly. "For good."

NEW TROUBLE

Despite Farmer Pat unexpectedly driving off, and the moment of shock it brought, in the twenty minutes he was gone the four friends regathered their optimism, and concluded that their plan to get Farmer Pat to go back to the farm was most likely going to succeed. However, their growing sense of hope was dealt a sharp new blow when Farmer Pat's truck returned a short while later towing a trailer.

"Here he comes – I knew he'd be back!" called Baz, excitedly. He had been acting as watch at the edge of the wall, his long neck perfect for stretching around the corner and taking quick looks. "But he has something behind his truck."

"It's how they move the horses," replied Sam, after looking for herself. "That's not good at all."

"Why isn't it good?" asked Baz, anxiously.

"It means Daisy will get back home long before we do," answered Sam.

"Well, then we just need to get into the trailer as well," said Robert.

"Robert, I could never sneak into the trailer," said Sam. "Farmer Pat would see me straight away. But you and Baz could."

"Oh, Sam, we need you back at the farm – to help us get the animals ready," replied Robert, this time not trying to hold in his fear. "You will just have to try."

"Yes! You will," added Baz, quickly. "We are all in this together."

"Robert, I promise you," said Sam, "it will ruin our plan if Farmer Pat finds me. He will make sure I am tied up properly this time. He might not even stay at the farm long enough for us to wake up the animals."

"Now I agree with Sam," said Baz.

"But what..." Sam went on, quickly. "What if I started for home right now? I think by the time he puts Daisy in the trailer, I might just be able to get back first. That way I could wake up the other animals before you arrive."

"I think... I mean..." began Robert, who was beginning to get flustered. "But are you sure you'll make it in time, Sam?"

"Sam, it's a very long way," added Baz. "I don't mean to be rude... I know sometimes I am..."

"Baz, I think these old legs can get me there," replied Sam, knowing what Baz was going to say. "I just need a good head start."

At this moment, Farmer Pat's truck began reversing the trailer into the driveway.

"We don't have any more time to waste, Robert," said Sam, urgently. "I think I should go."

Robert looked at Sam, then at Baz, trying to glean from their faces the best decision. "Baz, what is Farmer Pat doing right now - is he looking our way?"

Baz stretched his neck around the edge of the wall, then pulled it back in again. "No," he whispered.

"Okay, but are you sure, Sam?" said Robert. "Are you sure you'll be all right?"

"Yes, yes... I am," replied Sam, her voice trying to remain confident. "And... and... it has already been marvellous to have done this with you all. Those first few days after Hennie passed away were so..."

"Sam!" said Baz, his voice tightening. "You're making it sound as if it's over. Do not do that! We'll see you back at home in a little while. There is nothing more certain than this fact."

"Of course you will," replied Sam, putting her paw on Baz's back. "This plan will work – I agree it will - so you will see me soon."

"Yes, we will," added Robert. "Good luck, Sam."

"Good luck, Sammy," said Baz, doing his best to hide his shaking left leg.

With that, Sam crept out from behind the wall, then quickly across the other side of the road, and into the dark shadows under the tall pine trees. From this position of safety, she looked back at her friends, who saw this and waved at her. Sam waved back then hurried down the road.

Almost immediately, Robert and Baz heard the town's dogs beginning to bark.

"Oh, that's good," said Baz, relieved, "that's very good. The dogs are helping her again."

"Yes," Robert answered, his voice barely above a whisper with all the emotion it was carrying. "Now it's our turn, Baz. We need to get into the trailer."

"We should just show Farmer Pat that we are here. That would be much easier," Baz replied, catching Robert off guard by stepping out from behind the wall.

"Baz! Get back here!" called Robert.

"But I don't understand…" Baz said after crouching down again.

"It's because Farmer Pat might put us inside the truck," Robert went on quickly. "Then we'll be stuck. We are just going to have to jump onto the back edge of the trailer once he's ready to go."

"That little ledge?" replied Baz, looking at the small metal step sitting just below the trailer's doors.

"Yes. Then we'll leap off it at the other end before Farmer Pat can see us."

"Robert, that sounds very dangerous. The truck will be driving very fast. We might fall off."

"You can use your beak to hold on. You are always telling me how hard you can bite. My hands and feet have good grip."

"Okay," said Baz, after staring at Robert for a few long moments. He was still not sure this was a good idea, but he was also painfully aware that there were no other plans popping into his head.

Over the next ten minutes, as they watched Farmer Pat check the trailer inside and out, making it safe for Daisy, Robert began to feel slightly better again, and that their plan was back on track. This feeling only grew stronger when, in the far distance, there was another burst of dogs barking, but this time very faint, meaning Sam must now be near the far side of town. "I think she might make it home first," Robert said to Baz.

"I'll be honest, Robert, she can run faster than I thought she could," replied Baz.

Even Farmer Pat, who of course knew nothing of the plan, added to their sense that the plan had started out well, when he said to Daisy, "Do you know, girl, I have never known an easier time getting a cow into a trailer in my whole life." Which, as we know, was the truth; for Daisy, like most big animals, hated getting into trailers, but on this occasion she was doing her best to kick up the least fuss possible.

When she was finally in the trailer, she looked through its small window at her friends, then called out to them - nothing of which would have seemed strange to Farmer Pat; to him it would have only sounded like a quick "moo" - but it was enough for Baz and Robert to know she was all right and still as determined as they were for their plan to succeed.

WHAT DO WE DO?

Just a few minutes later, Farmer Pat's truck burst into life and rolled slowly out of the driveway until it reached the kerb, ready to turn into the street. This was Robert and Baz's moment. And it was Robert who gave the signal for the next part of their journey to begin, by calling out at the top of his voice, "Let's go, Baz! Let's get going!" Then he hopped at full speed from their hiding place towards the trailer's ledge.

If Robert had been at all worried he might have left Baz behind, he needn't have been; for, as he had often claimed, Baz was indeed a very fast waddler, and was quickly past Robert, reaching the back of the trailer first. Once there, he stretched up with his beak, gripped onto a small piece of welded metal, and used it to pull himself onto the trailer ledge.

When safely on board, Baz swung his head around to check on Robert.

"Robert! Get up here now!" he called urgently, seeing his friend was still a few big hops away, "I can feel the car moving forwards. Hurry!"

"I'm almost there, Baz!" Robert called back anxiously.

At this stage, the truck was still only inching forwards, and despite the air of urgency this stage of the endeavour was of course going to have, it still would have been reasonable for Baz to comfortably assume that with only a few hops to go, Robert would make it onto the ledge without any major problems.

But to Baz's utter horror, his assumption was completely wrong. For just as Robert's feet left the ground to begin his final leap onto the ledge, Farmer Pat's foot pressed down the truck's accelerator. The result was that the truck moved only a little further, but it was enough that, instead of landing on the ledge, Robert missed it completely and landed hard on the road.

When Robert looked up, shocked inside and out, the first thing he saw were Baz's disbelieving eyes. "Get up, Robert!" Baz bellowed at the top of his voice as he began to move away from Robert, not caring if anyone else would hear him. "Get up! Hurry up! You must catch up!"

But as the stunned Robert obeyed his friend's command and began hopping down the road, there was already a part of him which realised the truck was too far away and travelling too fast.

And when his hopping brought him no closer - indeed the gap was widening - he called out in a voice that was filled with a surprising strength, "Baz! You, Sam and Daisy must organise the animals! You have to do this. You will get Farmer Pat to stay. You can do it, Baz!"

"No, Robert!" Baz called back. "It's not possible. Keep hopping! Please!"

"Baz, I totally believe the three of you can do it," Robert answered, determined not to show any sign of weakness. "You don't need me!"

Baz had heard and clearly understood everything Robert was saying. And actually, for all the bravado and silly comments he was famous for, deep in his bones he mostly had a proper sense of the truth of things.

And this truth was telling him that what Robert was saying was impossible. No one was going to be able to get the animals to sing in the same way Robert could. And without that, there would not be the new music machine that Farmer Pat needed to hear. There was simply no point going back to the farm without Robert. So, even though it felt partly wrong, he let go his grip of the trailer and leapt from it, landing face first as Robert had, fifty metres up the road.

As Baz waddled towards him, Robert called out first, this time not trying to be brave or strong or wise, but letting out all his sorrow. "Baz, I'm so sorry I missed the jump... I don't know how I could have made such a mistake..."

"It's not your fault, Robert," replied Baz when he reached him, consoling his friend by opening up his wing and gathering him under it. "I felt the truck move, Robert. There was nothing more to it. I'm sorry, too, that I jumped off. I know you wanted me to stay. But we cannot do this task without you. You have to be at the farm, leading the animals. It's the only way. We need to get you back there."

"But, Baz, I think..." said Robert, feeling desperately sad, "it's hopeless. I really think it is this time."

"No. It's not," replied Baz, firmly. "We are not going to give up now, Robert. Not yet. We can't."

"Baz..."

"Robert. You have to listen to me. This is my turn to help you. Now, I want you to hop onto my back."

"Oh, Baz, it's... I... it's just... I don't think we have any chance of catching them," Robert finally got out, hating that he could not be more supportive of his friend. "No matter how fast you run."

These were honest words. It was true that no matter how hard Baz tried - and he could try very hard, as we learned at the beginning of the story when he chased away the fox - there was no chance he was ever going to waddle to the farm before Farmer Pat's truck reached it.

But there was more to the story. Far more to the story. For there was a hidden piece of it that Robert did not know, a piece which the sorrow of the last five minutes had brought to the surface and had led to a very serious conversation between Baz's head and his heart. One he could never have imagined taking place before that moment.

Baz knew there was a way they could catch up to Farmer Pat. Robert could not know, but Baz did. Indeed, no animal on the farm could have known, for it was Baz's secret.

And the secret was that Baz could actually fly. It was just that he had been so terribly scared of doing it ever since he had the accident when he was a duckling. But on this night, with everything at stake, he knew he could not live with himself if he did not now, at the very least, try to fly Robert back to Stone Hill Farm.

"Robert, please, hop on," Baz said firmly. "And hold on tight. I am going to need to run very fast."

"Baz!" replied Robert, becoming exasperated with his friend's refusal to accept the truth. "We are not going to be able to catch up to them."

"Robert, as a matter of fact, we definitely will be able to if... I... I..." began Baz, his heart beating so rapidly it stopped him from forming the right words.

"Baz... please..." said Robert, beginning to feel very sad.

"We will... we will be able to make it on time... if I... if I fly us back home."

"If you fly us?"

"Yes," replied Baz, feeling a shift inside himself, as though a mighty weight had fallen out of him along with his big secret. "I am going to fly you back home, Robert.

We are going to get Farmer Pat to stay, like we said we would."

"But, Baz, you can't fly," replied Robert, bewildered.

"I can. I just don't."

"When was the last time you flew, Baz? I have never seen you."

"A long time ago," replied Baz, all his terror of flying returning with a painful rush at the reality of what lay ahead of him. "What other choice do we have, Robert?"

The truth was, there was only one choice. They could try and fly back, or lose Farmer Pat forever - and with him, the life on the farm they loved so much.

"Baz," said Robert, after a long moment's silence as they both pondered their choice. "I think we can do this."

"I think we can too," Baz replied, even though at the same time another part of him felt it was impossible.

With this brief exchange, it was as though the two frightened friends agreed that further words would only do harm. So Baz simply folded his legs and dropped to the ground. Robert looked at Baz, smiled warmly, put his arm gently around his neck for a moment, then hopped onto his back and took a good hold of some of his feathers.

When Robert was safely aboard, Baz waddled into the middle of the road. But as he turned and looked down it, it suddenly became shockingly clear just how tall the pine trees that lined it were. Knowing he would need to fly that high over them filled him with new terror, and as he began waddling, all he could think to do to release some of this horrible terror was to start shouting, "All right! Let's fly, Baz! Up we go, Baz! Let's fly now!"

But in spite of these commands to himself, Baz only continued to waddle more quickly, directly down the street. It was then that Robert, who was nearly as scared as Baz, but not quite, took back command of the task at hand. "You need to start flapping your wings, Baz," he yelled. "Start flapping your wings!"

"I know, Robert! I know that's what I have to do," Baz yelled back, but to show how he was really feeling, he actually tightened his wings to his side.

"Start flapping them, Baz!" said Robert, leaning forwards and speaking directly into Baz's ear, while wedging his arms under the top of Baz's wings to help him open them.

"Okay!" replied Baz, still waddling as fast as he could. "Okay, I will!"

At this moment, a reasonable person would say these two animals, who were doing their best to try and help someone they loved, did not need, or deserve to face, another obstacle. Indeed, it would seem unnecessary and unkind, almost as though their good hearts and the intentions they carried were not being properly listened to by the Universe.

But if we are being fair, we cannot place the blame for this injustice on the driver of the car cresting over a hill ahead of them. For he could not possibly have known what they had already been through on this long night. And we must also have faith that if he had known of their struggles, he would have slowed down or even stopped to help them, rather than honking his horn and flashing his lights as he was doing at this moment, feeling it was an adequate warning to alert a duck to move to the side of the road.

"Robert, do you see that? There's a car coming!" called Baz over his shoulder. "We should definitely stop."

"No, no - not now," replied Robert, hiding his fear, for he instinctively knew that if they did stop, they would never start again. "We just need to get in the air and fly over it."

"But what happens if we can't?" said Baz, suddenly almost in tears.

"We can! You can," implored Robert quietly. "Just start flapping your wings, Baz."

"Robert... please..."

"You can do it, Baz. You can!" yelled Robert, strongly. "We need you to do it now, Baz. We all need you to be a hero."

"Yes, a hero," said Baz to himself. It was the right word for the right occasion, and he let it burst into the very core of him. And it did something. It changed something, giving his fear one final shove out of the way. And with it gone, Baz unfurled his wings and started flapping them as fast as he could.

"Good, Baz, good!" yelled Robert.

"Okay, okay, okay, okay..." Baz called back, at the top of voice, which could now only just be heard over the urgent honking of the car horn.

"You need to jump, Baz!" yelled Robert at the top of his voice. "You need to jump and flap at the same time."

"Jump! Flap! Jump and FLAP!" Baz called out again.

And with that he concentrated every part of his being into flying, and suddenly, almost miraculously, he felt himself lift from the ground, his feet clipping the car's windscreen.

In an instant, the incredibly close brush with injury was forgotten... for Baz was already being filled with the most enormous feeling of exhilaration.

"I am flying, Robert," he called as much to the Universe as to Robert.

"I know, Baz," Robert called back. "I'm flying too!"

What a sight it would have been for any birds or insects who might see these two friends flying for the first time. They still faced many potential problems, such as Robert falling off, or being spotted by a bird of prey who would not believe their luck that there, most peculiarly, perched on the back of a duck, was one of their favourite meals. And most pressing of all were the hard, unanswered questions around Baz's ability to land. But at that moment, the two friends were utterly captivated by what they were experiencing.

And for a few minutes they said nothing. They merely looked up at the stars and the moon, which seemed to be that far closer - almost as though, if they had the time and were able to fly just a little higher, it could be reached and touched, and perhaps even plucked from the air to help explain to their friends the feelings they had experienced on this first wonderful, magical flight.

It wasn't until Robert spotted Sam far below that this flood of joy and euphoria gave way to the practical once more.

"There's Sam!" called Robert excitedly. "Just down there, on the edge of the road, can you see her?"

"I really do not want to look down, Robert," replied Baz.

"She's still a long way from the farm," replied Robert, seeing the house sitting atop the Steep Hill in the far distance. It reminded him of the reality and difficulty of the task ahead.

"Can you see Farmer Pat and Daisy?"

"Yes, I think so," replied Robert, spotting the lights of the only car on the road up ahead. "If it's them, he's still a good way ahead of Sam, though, Baz."

"That's not good, Robert," Baz replied, one word at a time, between deep breaths.

"No. No, it's not," said Robert, all manner of new problems running through him. "Baz, I don't think Sam is going to make it to the farm before Farmer Pat does. We are going to have to move the animals up to Farmer Pat's house ourselves."

"How on earth are we going to do that?" replied Baz. "The Pond Paddock gate is locked and the big animals won't be able to get through it."

"Then we will just have to make do with whoever can make it. It might still work."

"Robert, you know we need everyone. That's what you have always told us."

"Baz," Robert replied after a moment, "there might be another way."

"There is?"

"We are just going to have to convince everyone to climb up the Steep Hill."

"Robert!" Baz answered, exasperated. His wings stopped a little as a result, causing them to dip.

"Baz! Keep flapping!"

"But no one has ever climbed it, Robert," Baz finally said. "Except you. They will not do it."

"It's the only way left now," replied Robert, feeling deeply worried again, for he knew Baz was almost certainly right to have these doubts. But at the same time - the same awful time - there simply did not seem to be another way left to them.

"EVERYONE NEEDS TO HURRY!"

Even if this new task of getting all the animals from the Pond to the house felt too hard for the two friends, one piece of good news arrived with it: having to fly down to the Pond meant they could also use it to land on.

This, of course, meant that if Baz were to misjudge anything (and even he would have admitted that was likely) and were to crash-land, being a duck and a frog, they would both be protected by the water and be able to swim to safety.

Perhaps this was why, when minutes later they passed over the top of the truck on the road, then onto the property itself, and approached the Pond below them, Baz relaxed slightly for the first time on the flight. And when his feet hit the water not far from the edge of the

157

Pond, he managed to control his feet and wings to such an extent that he skidded to a stop just a small distance from the edge.

This landing was so remarkably perfect that, when it was combined with his years of practice waddling out of the Pond at high speed, he was able to step straight onto the soft sandy beach in one motion.

"Incredible, Baz. Just incredible!" said Robert, leaping off Baz's back. These words sent an arrow of such good feeling through Baz that for the first time in his life, he could not think of anything to say in response.

But as it happened, he did not need to say anything, because standing on the edge of the Pond, getting some fresh morning water into her children, was Mrs Crichett. She filled the silence with her appalled but deeply confused expression, which said more than Baz could have ever come up with at that moment. Then she finally spluttered, "What...?"

"I can explain..." began Baz.

"No, I can explain!" Mrs Crichett fired back, all doubt about what to say having exited her body during the spluttering. "All these years of jumping onto other animals' backs and waddling around claiming you couldn't fly!"

"Sorry, Mrs Crichett," replied Baz, walking straight past her, "but we can't stop right now."

"Oh, yes, you will stop, young man!" she replied, chasing after him, on a mission to grab him by his tail feathers. "And what's with this 'we' business? You are going to face up to this on your own..."

"Mrs Crichett," called Robert urgently. "Stop! Please wait just a moment and listen to us!"

"Oh, goodness, Robert, you're caught up in this too?" she honked out, spinning around. "You should know better after all this time! When I am finished with this fool, you and I shall have a very serious conversation about your friendships, for you have been led quite astray!"

"Mrs Crichett…" replied Robert, with a sudden seriousness in his voice. "Please stop for just a moment. I know this looks all wrong. I promise you there is a proper explanation for all of this. We can explain everything later. But right now, we desperately need your help."

"My help? Oh, I don't think so. You've already had it, Robert. And look where it has led you."

"Yes. I know I have, Mrs Crichett. And your help made a world of difference. You just don't know it yet. But what you are seeing - us flying - is still all about Farmer Pat," Robert continued. "He is on his way back here right this minute."

"Farmer Pat? On his way back?" she replied, after a moment. "I don't think so, Robert… he is gone now."

Then for the first time in the whole night - or so it seemed to Robert - a moment arrived which did not make things harder, rather more helpful. For just after Mrs Crichett said "gone now", Farmer Pat's truck drove around the last bend in the road, and stopped, its lights shining brightly through the front gates.

"Baz, they're here already," said Robert, pointing at the gate, with a clear note of fear in his voice.

"We need to hurry, Robert," replied Baz. "We need to start waking up the other animals right now."

"Mrs Crichett," said Robert, "as you can see, we have been able to get Farmer Pat back to the farm. This is what we have been doing all night. This is why Baz is suddenly flying. And why I was on his back. But Farmer Pat is not going to stay here unless we get all the animals to the top of the Steep Hill and we sing for him."

"All the way to the top of the Steep Hill?" she replied after a long moment of consideration, but with a softness in her voice that no one, except perhaps her children when sick, would have ever heard before. "But, Robert, most of us have never been up there before."

"I know that," Robert replied. "I know that, Mrs Crichett. But I have. And if I can do it, so can everybody else. But we just have to get everyone up the Steep Hill before Farmer Pat leaves."

And as he said this, as though he had the power to make utterly certain Mrs Crichett understood how serious the situation was, the car lights began moving again, and for just a moment they shone directly down the valley, lighting the faces of the three animals. In that moment, any last reservations Mrs Crichett may have still had were banished by the utter sincerity and concern she saw on the faces of the two animals.

"Look, Robert!" said Baz, alarmed, and pointing his wing which, as the excitement of flying began to wear off, was now shaking. "Farmer Pat is already through the gates and onto the road to the house."

"Yes... I can see..." said Robert, a horrible feeling forming in his stomach. "Mrs Crichett? Can..."

"And there's Sam!" interrupted Baz, joyfully. "There's Sam, she's made it back."

"Is that really Sam?" asked Mrs Crichett, her sense of astonishment and confusion mingling together and making any clear thought nearly impossible.

"Yes, it is Sam," replied Robert. "I promise."

Then, as if to remove any doubt in Mrs Crichett's mind, Sam started barking.

"Oh, it is Sam," she said. "But what is she doing all the way over there? Why isn't she up at the house?"

"Mrs Crichett, she has been with us all night," replied Robert. "She came with us to the Big Town."

"The Big Town? All that way?"

"Yes, to get Farmer Pat. Now she's trying to tell Farmer Pat to go to the house, so that he doesn't just put Daisy in the Pond Paddock then leave again."

"Oh... I see," said Mrs Crichett, to no one in particular, but with a tone suggesting there was no room left in her mind for any new information. Then, as though losing a clear sense of what she was going to do next, she returned to deeply familiar patterns, and turned and took a few slow steps away from the Pond's edge, seemingly heading home.

"Mrs Crichett!" called Robert, alarmed. "Where are you going? We need your help."

"I know, Robert," she called back, turning her head. "And although this climb is quite the most peculiar thing

I have ever heard of, there is not a moment to waste, is there?"

And with that, she set off at a cracking pace, her children hot on her heels, honking at the top of her tremendously loud voice, "Everybody up! Not a moment to waste! There is always time to sleep! Get up! Get up! Everybody up! It's an emergency. We all need to get to the top of the Steep Hill. Yes, you heard me correctly. To the top of the Steep Hill."

SAM AND
FARMER PAT

If the breeze had been stronger and coming from a different direction, Farmer Pat would have certainly heard Mrs Crichett's honking, and wondered to himself if there was a fox or snake moving dangerously close to her goslings. Not that it would have raised too great an alarm in him about the safety of her little ones, for on more than one occasion, just like Baz's tail, his own boots and ankles had been on the receiving end of Mrs Crichett's snapping beak; so he knew it would be a foolhardy fox to take her on.

But even if favourable winds had been pushing Mrs Crichett's voice to him, there still would not have been any guarantee she would have been heard, for Sam's loud persistent barking had not stopped or dropped in intensity since she had finally caught up to the truck.

"Sam! Sam! Stop!" called Farmer Pat out the window for the third or fourth time at least. "What are you barking at, girl? You've got it all jumbled up. I am truly sorry I left you behind. But it was only for a few days. Didn't you think I was coming back for you? It was just until I found my new home. That's all. Not forever."

When these words didn't soothe her, he reached over, opened the passenger side door, and called out, "C'mon, girl, in you get. It's your favourite spot. Let me give you a big pat. I think that would be a good idea for everyone."

Sam would normally have regarded this invitation as a golden chance to have a ride in the truck's front seat, one of her greatest pleasures. But this time, she ignored its call and continued to bark at the truck, saying over and over, "We need you up at the house, Farmer Pat. You must come to the house. Do not just drop Daisy back in the paddock and leave again."

This was all very confusing for Farmer Pat, for he had never known Sam to be like this. Certainly, he had never known her to refuse a ride in the truck. So instead of getting mad, he continued trying to gently calm her down, telling her again and again, "I was always coming back for you, Sammy. Don't think for a moment I could ever leave you behind. But, you see, I don't even know where I am going."

But of course, no matter how kind or warm Farmer Pat was to her, Sam was never going to stop barking. So in the end, when he realised Sam was not going to relent, he eventually gave up, restarted the engine, then continued down the driveway toward the Pond Paddock turn-off to unload Daisy from the trailer.

But if he was secretly wishing that Sam would eventually wear herself out and calm down on her own accord, this hope was soon dashed as well. For when Farmer Pat did turn onto the Pond Paddock track, and Sam knew her barking was not going to be enough, she took the far more serious risk of darting in front of the truck and biting the front tyres.

For a person as kind as Farmer Pat, this was the final straw. The last thing in the world he wanted was for Sam to be injured. So he slammed on the brakes, opened the door, climbed out, and then, rather than chasing her, he crouched down and began calling to her, "Sammy, please, under no circumstances do I want you getting hurt. Are you hungry? Is that it? How about I take you back up and give you some of your favourite biscuits? And some fresh water?"

All this confused action in the Pond Paddock had taken a good deal of time. Enough time, in fact, for Robert to have been carried a good distance up the Steep Hill on the back of one of the goats. Now he was almost at the top and had leapt onto a large rock, which was giving him the perfect view of Sam and Farmer Pat, along with the climbing animals. Except for the most fearful, they had

165

all been successfully roused and motivated out of their slumber by Mrs Crichett.

As he took his eye off Sam and Farmer Pat for a moment and watched the animals climbing, Robert soon noticed some beautiful patterns. The animals that were scared or finding the climb too hard were being helped, and sometimes carried, by the bigger ones; the more agile ones were climbing ahead and calling out to the others below them things such as, "Watch out for that low branch - it has thorns on it," or, "This rock looks like it is about to roll down the hill."

And if the rock was small enough, the animals who were big and strong enough to push it, called out, "Everyone watch out!" And they rolled it down the hill before anyone could be seriously hurt, as would have been the case if it were to suddenly tumble down on its own accord.

It was an inspiring and moving sight for Robert to see. But as exciting and hopeful as it was, the hopeful feelings only increased when, after watching the truck drive back up the path, he saw Sam and Farmer Pat turning left onto the driveway instead of right, which meant they were now heading towards the house.

As he looked back and forth between the animals and Farmer Pat's truck, Robert allowed himself the precious thought that, against all odds, the "big idea" which had arrived from the very centre of his heart, might be going to work. If all the animals could just make it to the top of the Steep Hill and sing, Farmer Pat might be convinced to stay after all. "It's going to be close," he whispered to himself, "very close. But if everything works, I think there is just enough time to hide and be ready before Farmer Pat arrives."

But just as this thought was reducing the tension that had taken over his body, in the distance he saw the truck suddenly stop in the middle of the driveway, for no clear reason. Then, adding to Robert's confusion, a few moments later, Farmer Pat got out of the truck, walked a short distance up the driveway, and sat on an old tree stump. "What is he doing?" Robert said to himself, filled with a sudden sense of dread. "Why is he stopping there?"

These were the exact same feelings a terribly worried Sam was dealing with, as she stood a few metres from Farmer Pat, watching on as he stared up at the house, not moving or saying anything. Farmer Pat didn't even react when Sam began barking again, saying to him, "We need you up at the house, Farmer Pat. Everyone is there waiting for you. There's a beautiful surprise."

It was even more troubling when Sam ventured closer, barking more softly, then whining, and finally nudging his hands repeatedly with her nose, saying, "We all love you and want you to stay here with us." For he remained motionless, his eyes fixed on the house on top of the Steep Hill.

As a last step, Sam lay her head in Farmer Pat's lap and was very still. For a few moments, Farmer Pat also remained still. Then finally he sighed deeply and said, as much to himself as to Sam, "I'm sorry, girl. I know you want me to go back up there. But I just can't without Hennie."

With that, he stroked her head and neck softly and said, "And I'm so sorry I left you behind, Sammy. You can come with me now. I'm not even sure where I am going to yet. But I won't ever leave you behind again. That I promise."

ONE LAST CHANCE

As Robert watched Sam put his head on Farmer Pat's lap, he could not make the slightest sense of what was happening. "Why did Sam stop barking?" he said out loud to himself, in a way that also sounded as if he was addressing the question to the Universe, hoping that having known and seen so much, it had an answer. "Why is she just lying next to Farmer Pat? There's no reason Sam would suddenly go against everything we had planned."

However, when Robert saw Farmer Pat leading Sam by the collar to the truck, his heart began beating quickly, for he once again allowed himself to think, "They are still heading up to the house after all." But this new hope was gone moments later when, after getting into the truck, Farmer Pat began turning it, and the trailer, around. This time Robert knew that once he had locked Daisy in the paddock, he would be leaving the farm for good.

It was a heartbreaking moment for Robert. And it was all the more so, because he could see a group of the goats making their way over The Giant's Teeth, almost as though they were walking on flat ground. He could also see other groups of animals not far behind them. "We are so close! We are so close!" he said furiously to himself, which caused some of the animals nearby to look at him. "We cannot just let Farmer Pat leave."

It was then Robert saw Baz standing on top of one of The Giant's Teeth.

"Baz! Baz!"

"Robert?" Baz called back, not immediately seeing his small friend, and scanning the slope of the Steep Hill for him. "Where are you? I can't see you."

"I'm down below, look right near the edge!"

"Keep talking!"

"Baz! Over here! Baz!"

"Oh! I see you!" Baz finally called down excitedly, seeing his friend. "Look at us up here! We are almost there. It's almost done. Can you believe it, Robert?"

"Baz, it's not almost done! Farmer Pat is leaving again," Robert called, pointing to the truck winding its way along the driveway. "This time with Sam as well. They're not coming to the farmhouse."

"Oh... it can't be," said Baz to himself, dropping down, his legs giving way. Like Robert moments before, he was being struck with the worst feeling that any animal or human can feel, which is when something so deep or valuable, so essential to the way we feel about the world, begins to appear lost. This was the feeling that Robert and Baz were dealing with.

"It's not over, Baz," called Robert, strongly, gathering himself. "We are not giving up now. We just can't, Baz. You need to get down here!"

"Robert, but can't you see?" called Baz, looking at the truck, then back at Robert, "They're almost gone. It's hopeless."

"We have one last chance to try and get him to turn around," Robert replied. "We have to fly to the gate."

"Fly... again?" said Baz, the last word getting stuck in his throat before finally being forced out.

"Baz, I will never ask you to fly ever again if you try this one last time."

"Oh, Robert..." The waver in Baz's voice told Robert just how scared he was.

"Oh, Baz... but what else can we do?"

"Nothing, Robert... there's nothing else we can do," Baz replied after a long moment, during which Robert did not know if his friend was going to answer yes or no to their last hope.

But then Baz, feeling deeply unsteady inside and outside, provided the answer to the question by slowly getting to his feet, and calling in a tight tone, "I'm coming down to you, Robert. As a start. That's all I can promise."

"We can do this, Baz. I know we can," Robert replied.

With that, Baz took a series of flapping hops down across the rocks until he was by Robert's side, standing so close that his trembling legs knocked into Robert's side.

171

"Do you think you can do it, Baz?" Robert asked, quietly. "I'm scared, too, if that helps."

"Don't tell me that!" replied Baz, still not moving. "I only have one thought in my mind, Robert. It's that you had better climb on to my back before I become even more frightened. Because if that happens..."

"Baz," replied Robert, climbing on Baz's back, "let's go and catch Farmer Pat and Sam."

"Yes... let's do that!" yelled Baz, some of his old bravado suddenly returning.

When Baz felt his friend's grip tighten around his neck, he took three deep breaths, then three big steps, and leapt off the edge of the Steep Hill.

Moments later, incredible as it might seem for a duck who had only learned to fly that very day, Baz was sweeping down the side of the Steep Hill, over the farm's deepest valley, along which the road to the house wound. It was then that Robert had the feeling that on this incredible night, with all that had happened, they most likely only had one last final piece of luck left to them. And understanding that they needed to make sure of it, he leant forward to Baz's ear to tell him the details of their last plan.

"Baz, I think we are going to need to land on Farmer Pat's truck."

"Land on Farmer Pat's truck! Why?"

"Otherwise he might never see us."

"That sounds very, very dangerous, Robert. And very, very hard. We could very easily be..."

"I don't think we have a choice, Baz," interrupted Robert, not wanting the worst thoughts of this plan to be said out loud, as though not saying them might somehow help prevent them.

"Oh, Robert, don't say that. I don't like the sound of that at all."

Whether they had a choice or not, one thing was quite certain. A decision was going to be needed in the next few moments, because just ahead of them, Farmer Pat was out of his truck, and was beginning to close the heavy wooden gate one final time.

The sight had a profound, jolting sense on Baz, and he called out, his voice full of fear, "I'm going to try to land on the truck, Robert. For you, me, Daisy and Sam, I am going to try."

"That's magnificent, Baz," said Robert quietly, hanging on with all his strength, having no way of knowing what was about to happen to them both, but with the faith that after all they had been through and survived, somehow he and Baz would make it through.

Seconds later, as Farmer Pat climbed into his truck and started the engine, Baz swooped down, wings flapping frantically in reverse to slow them down, and hit the bonnet feet first in the same way as if he was landing on water.

But they had come in far too fast, and much too low, and when they hit the slippery truck bonnet, despite Baz attempting to flap even harder in reverse, they skidded straight across the bonnet, crashed off the other side, and landed hard on the gravelly road, then rolled into some bushes.

Inside the truck, Farmer Pat had the shock of his life. Like most farmers, he had never known a duck, of all things, to try and land on the bonnet of his truck.

But before he had a chance to make any further sense of yet another act of strange animal behaviour, Sam suddenly began barking furiously again and scratching the windscreen. "Sam! What is it this time? What have you seen, girl? Can you see the poor duck? C'mon, let's go and see if it's hurt itself."

But just as he was reaching across Sam to open her door, Farmer Pat heard the shrill but familiar sound of a frog croaking. And when he looked ahead to find out who was making the sound, he saw a frog with a blue stripe running across the top of its head, standing in the headlights directly in front of him, trying to block his way.

"Robert?" was all Farmer Pat could get out, feeling as if he had been plucked from the ground and turned upside down by a giant, such was his disorientation. He only felt more so when, moments later, Baz limped out of the bushes and dropped down next to Robert.

At this moment, Farmer Pat finally understood that the events of the night were something far beyond his loyal dog, Sam, and favourite cow, Daisy, wanting to come with him to his new home. He saw a pattern to the rhythms of this night: that the animals were trying to tell him something deeply important, and in his terrible sadness over losing Hennie, he had forgotten to say a proper goodbye to a group of animals he loved, and who loved him with all their hearts.

"Sammy," he finally said, putting his hand on her back, "I am going to stay for tonight, girl. What say we do one last morning on the tractor and I say goodbye to all these beautiful, marvellous animals? I don't know what I was thinking, just going off like I did without saying a proper farewell."

HOME

Not long afterwards, Farmer Pat and the four friends pulled up outside The Stone House. When Farmer Pat opened the car door, Sam leapt over his lap and began pulling on his trouser leg. And if there was one thing Farmer Pat had learned this night, it was to listen to his animals, so he happily let Sam lead him to his favourite chair on the porch.

"You're not going to make me a cup of tea too, are you, girl?" he said, his voice wavering slightly, for the love he was feeling from these animals was stirring feelings in him that he had been trying to keep away ever since Hennie had passed away. "I wouldn't put anything past you all tonight."

As these feelings made their way through Farmer Pat's body, Robert climbed onto a big boulder that sat in the middle of the yard. Although it had been sitting there for a period of time too vast for humans to properly grasp, at the same time it looked as though it had been placed there moments before for this specific purpose; for it was the perfect size and height for a small frog to be seen by others.

Once firm on his feet and feeling sure of himself, Robert called, "Everyone! Farmer Pat is here. Come out!" In answer to this, the animals - who numbered well over a hundred - emerged from their hiding places inside and behind the barn, and slowly surrounded the big boulder.

To Farmer Pat, sitting on his porch, this sudden gathering of all the animals on the home plateau, of all places, was the most miraculous happening he had ever seen. "Sam... what is going on here? Is this everyone? How could it be, Sam? How did they get here? And why? Strange things have been occurring at such a pace I can hardly believe I am awake."

Robert sensed Farmer Pat's puzzlement and bewilderment most of all. And as he watched the animals gather around him, he was wondering if indeed all the work and dreaming of the last week was going to affect Farmer Pat in the way that he, more than anything - and now more than ever - hoped it would.

With a mixture of hope and fear running through his head, Robert looked around the sea of faces. They were all there, including Baz, Daisy, Lucy, Charlie, and, of course, Mrs Crichett. And he was reassured, for he found them full of concentration, intent and joy, which in turn gave him the strongest sense that each animal knew this was going to be the very best they were ever going to be able to sing this piece of music, and it was going to be an occasion to be stored in their hearts forever. And when Robert saw this, he felt such a calm and steadiness that he knew it was the signal to start the music.

"Are we ready?" he called out, quietly.

"Yes," came the reply, in near unison.

With that, Robert raised his arms, then dropped them.

Once the five notes were released from the bodies of the animals, they combined with the air and the view of the valley - which now had the beginning of the rising sun's light shining through - and created what can only be described as perfect music. It was music created by, and with, an energy that delivered life.

At the centre of it, Robert was singing and conducting with every last bit of energy he had. And as it neared the end, he even dared the thought, "Perhaps this piece of music has, by some unknown magic, come into its most beautiful imaginable form, surpassing, for a moment or two, the music he had once heard on the music machine."

When the last note had moved through the air into Farmer Pat, Robert opened his eyes and looked across at Farmer Pat's face. This was when he found the true answer to their music's worth, for tears were falling down his cheeks.

What followed was a long, peaceful silence which was finally broken by the scraping of Farmer Pat's chair as he leant forward and stroked Sam's head. "Good girl,

Sammy. You're a beautiful girl. C'mon, let's go and join the others."

Moments later, Farmer Pat was with the animals, who moved apart as he approached in such a way that Farmer Pat was soon in their middle, surrounded on all sides. In this close circle he was told by each of them, in their own way, how important he was to them; and equally, just how important it was for him to stay at Stone Hill Farm, and that they were his family as well.

"Thank you," Farmer Pat said, time and time again, his voice barely above a whisper, as he went around the group patting and stroking each of them in turn. "I want to thank all of you."

Robert was still standing on his boulder, watching on intently as Farmer Pat stood there with tears freely running down his face. But Robert, who knew much about sadness and loss, recognised something about the tears which made them different from the earlier ones. There was a happiness in them now as well.

Then Farmer Pat turned to Robert, and said, "I do not know how you have done it, my little friend. I do not know, and probably never will. But you always did have something special about you. And you have given me something I will treasure to the end of my days."

Robert could not understand the words Farmer Pat was saying. But when Farmer Pat extended his hand to Robert, Robert hopped onto it, in much the same way the yellow bird had done so many months before, and he understood their meaning.

Robert also felt with utter certainty that the music from the Stone House on the Steep Hill would once more roll its way down to the Pond on warm evenings, and that Farmer Pat understood there could never be a home for him other than this one.

With a sense of deep happiness and relief, Robert hopped from Farmer Pat's hand onto Daisy's back, where a smiling Baz was standing with his wing out, ready to bring him close.

"Robert, we did it," said Baz.

"Yes, Baz, we did," replied Robert, his voice barely above a whisper. "What has happened is a good thing. A very good thing."

"It was like magic, Robert," added Daisy, turning her head around to look at them.

"Yes, it was, Daisy," replied Robert. "It was a wonder."

With that, the three friends went to find Sam, who was somewhere amongst all the other animals, who were now talking excitedly amongst themselves. More than anything they wanted to celebrate and talk about the remarkable events of the last few weeks - events they knew they were sure to be talking about when they were old and grey and still listening to the music as it wound its way down the Steep Hill into their special Cave.

EPILOGUE

A few months after this wondrous night, Robert was perched on his favourite branch, watching as Farmer Pat's blue tractor - long since back into its familiar daily rhythm - meandered down the bumpy path towards the Pond.

One new addition to the old routine, however, was that the tractor was now being chased daily by Mrs Crichett's teenage goslings, who loved nothing more than to get their morning seed from Farmer Pat. And the feeling was mutual, as was evident by the way Farmer Pat laughed and called out to them, "Oh, back again, are we? Have you really eaten all yesterday's already? I was sure I brought double."

As Robert dreamily watched this morning's routine unfold, his attention was suddenly brought into sharper focus when he caught sight of Baz flying through the tops of a group of tall trees, before sweeping low over Farmer

Pat's head, then splashing onto the Pond. "That's odd," Robert said out loud. "Baz is normally still asleep at this hour."

"Robert!" Baz called out. "Robert!"

"Baz, I'm up here! What is it?" Robert called down. "You look exhausted."

"That's because I am! When I was flying yesterday, the wind suddenly changed direction. It was terrible. It pushed me all the way up to the lakes in the Far Mountains. I didn't think I would ever make it home again. My legs were shaking in such a horrible way…"

"Baz, slow down, take a breath. I can hardly understand you," replied Robert, who was beginning to get a strong feeling deep inside himself. "You were at the Far Mountains?"

"Yes, Robert… I have just been over there," he repeated more slowly, pointing with his wing as if showing the mountain to Robert would somehow make it more believable that he had flown such a long way. "Robert, when I was there… I was helped by a family of frogs. And the frogs all had the same blue stripes on their heads as you."

"Baz," replied Robert, his body beginning to tremble the same as Baz's legs, "are you sure?"

"Yes, Robert… and they told me that they had lost one of their sons in a storm a long time ago."

"That is what they said? Baz, are you completely sure?" said Robert, suddenly feeling that he might topple from the branch. "What did they look like? What did they say?"

"They looked like you, Robert. Just like you!"

For a long moment, Robert said nothing, before finally saying in the quietest of voices, "Baz, I had given up hope I would ever see them again."

"I know you had, Robert," replied Baz just as quietly, "but I can take you there. You could see them for yourself. To find out if they are your family and that it's not just a mistake or coincidence. We could go tomorrow morning as soon as the sun rises. Would you like that?"

"Yes," replied Robert. "Yes. I would like that very much, Baz."

＊

The following morning, after a long, restless night full of the most difficult and confusing dreams, Robert found himself flying on Baz's back, which was something he never thought he would do again. This time, however, there was no need to implore or encourage. This time, Baz knew exactly what he was doing and where he was going.

And after a long, tiring journey, Baz and Robert found themselves circling above one of the Far Mountains' lakes.

"Robert," called Baz, "you see the rocks in the reeds? That's where the frogs live. That's their home."

"I know, Baz," replied Robert, his eyes filling with tears.

"You do?" answered Baz, tentatively.

"Yes, Baz, this is where I used to live."

"Oh, I knew it!" replied Baz, feeling like laughing and crying at the same time. "If you are certain, then we are going to land."

"Yes, yes – I am certain, Baz!" replied Robert, gripping Baz even tighter. "You are the most wonderful friend, Baz, bringing me here."

What a sight it must have been for the animals of the Far Mountains Lake, to look up and see a small frog riding on the back of a duck slowly descending from the sky. But it would have looked less strange for one family of frogs, because Baz was already known to them. And what's more, at this moment, he was being seen through their eyes as a returning hero. For just one day earlier, this warm, friendly duck had told them he thought he knew where their missing son was, and promised he would bring him back as soon as he was able to.

Soon after, Baz and Robert landed safely and began quickly paddling to the rocks, where the whole frog family - a mother, father and their children – were all waiting, pointing, hugging, calling with pure joy, and wanting to dive into the water and swim to Baz. They barely dared to believe that after all this time, their beloved lost son and brother had found his way home to them.

But when Baz and Robert were close enough, it was Robert who could not wait any longer, and he dove from Baz's back, swimming as fast as he could to the rocks. This time there was no wild river to drag him under or away, and he was soon scrambling onto the rocks into the middle of his family. "Mum, Dad..." was all he could say as they surrounded him, holding him in tight, not wanting to ever let him go.

"Baz, you've brought our son back," said Robert's father joyfully, when an out-of-breath Baz finally struggled onto the rocks. "How... how can we ever thank you?"

"Oh, it's Robert who needs to be thanked," replied Baz, quickly becoming caught up in all the emotion, and joining in the hugging group. "He saved our home. It was quite the most incredible thing. You should all come and visit us. And hear us. We're quite marvellous!"

"Oh, that sounds like it would be a wonderful adventure, Baz," answered Robert's mother, holding Robert, not quite daring to believe it was him standing next to her.

"And I can fly you all!" replied Baz, grinning at Robert. "I would love to do that. Really, I would. Wouldn't I, Robert?"

"Yes, yes, you would, Baz," replied Robert, smiling happily, tears in his eyes, looking from his friend to his family, and back again, marvelling at the deep wonder of things that he had been returned to his family under these most unlikely of circumstances.

✳

Baz's promises from this day proved to be unlike so many others said in moments of great excitement and emotion, which are full of good intention and feeling but impossible to live up to when real life and its demands return. For over the next weeks, months and years, Baz made many trips, for music, adventure and love, between Stone Hill Farm and the Far Mountains, more often than not carrying on his back his great, dear friend, Robert the Frog.